Around
the
Block

Rob Durham

Kim,
I hope you enjoy.
It means the world
that you support my
dream career!

:)

Rob
Durham

Published and printed in the United States of America

This is a work of fiction. Names, characters, businesses, places, events, locales, and incidents are either the products of the author's imagination or used in a fictitious manner. Any resemblance to actual persons, living or dead, or actual events is purely coincidental.

ISBN-13: 978-0-692-09625-3

ACKNOWLEDGMENTS

I would like to thank Beth, my wife, for her constant support throughout this book's entire process.

Thank you to my consulting editor, Brittany Freeman, for her hard work, especially on the early drafts.
Thank you to Justin Leuthauser, Jack Lafferty and my other beta readers for their attention and feedback.
Thank you to my editors Kari Vo and Ethan James Clarke.
Thank you to my cover designers Ryan Kendall and Peggy Nehmen.
Thank you to my students, especially the 2016 fall creative writing class, for your feedback and motivation.

Well I took off running at the greatest speed
I didn't bother looking to either side of me
Well I didn't see, I just didn't see
What was really going on

—Isaac Brock, Modest Mouse

1

That February morning smelled like pig manure. Most days an eastern breeze blows the stench of cow into town, but that morning was one of those rare pig winds provided by the farm to the west. The sky still favored black over gray, and the cold air passed right through the sleeves of my favorite ratty sweatshirt. I started my run down South Street toward my usual route, oblivious to the nearby hand-scripted message that would transform my junior year.

I rounded the brown clumps of ice that were once mountains of plowed snow, and headed left up Main. My distorted reflection jogged alongside me in the shop windows. "Too skinny for a large, but a little too tall for a medium" was how my coaches always described me. The photographer who took my yearbook photo suggested I grow my hair out a little longer until my face caught up with my ears. None of these unflattering descriptions encouraged my hope of ever finding a girlfriend.

Our town had three stoplights, but at this hour I could jog straight through the intersections. The only corner showing any life was the one with the gas station. Inside, Pond Bridge's bored-out-of-his-mind police officer was chatting with the cashier. Most people didn't even lock their doors at night, especially on the southern side of town where there wasn't much to steal. If someone broke into my home, all they'd score was an out-of-date laptop and some 5K trophies. A majority of the residents owned some sort of firearm, but those were for sport. The mayor considered having a Groundhog Day celebration a few weeks ago, but the general consensus was that groundhogs were for target practice, not predicting screwy Ohio weather.

At the next block I hurdled a puddle and passed Perky's, the official coffee shop of Pond Bridge and the only business open later than the average teenage curfew. It used to be a bookstore, but I don't think enough people around here read. Across the alley from Perky's was a travel agency. While most of the population wasn't keen on getting out of Pond Bridge except for the occasional trip to the Wal-Mart over in Perry, a few families managed to see the world, or at least a beach in the Gulf they visited with a Groupon. Those "wealthier" folk all lived in the northern neighborhoods where the tougher part of my run started.

Houses and SUVs were much bigger on those streets, and the pavement wasn't as cracked. The street names alluded to some sort of forestry like Whispering Woods or Cedar Springs. Some of the driveways had glass backboards on their hoops, and a few garages were even three cars wide. If we lived up here, Dad would've been the only teacher in a five-block radius.

This is the area I spotted her a couple weeks ago: a female runner emerging from an alley a block away. I barely saw her. It was dark, and for all I know she could've been one of my classmates' mothers. But in my lonely fantasy, she was the perfect girl who liked to get up and run every morning. She was looking for a guy like me to share the sunrise with. She would make the first move. She would reach out to me. She would understand how shy I was and she'd appreciate it. She just needed to reappear in the same way. But each morning I became more unsure of myself. Maybe she'd been a mirage. An illusion invented by my hormones in the way thirst tricks someone into seeing an oasis or a student hears of snow flurries and pictures a blizzard. Imaginary or not, I'd have a better track season from the extra training.

I always hung a right on the last street in town. Turning left would take me out on Edge Road which became a county highway with almost no space to run on the shoulder. "Stay off of Edge Road. Too many crazy drivers," Mom used to say. Even at seventeen I still respected her wishes. Instead, I always ran east past my best friend Brian's house. A few of the other guys I hang out with lived in the area, but they'd never get up early. Or run.

When I reached the eastern border of Pond Bridge, I took another right to return south towards my final stop, the cemetery. Its iron gate was permanently rusted open, and the trees were always a season ahead. The maple by Mom's grave showed colorful buds. They looked like painted nails on the fingers of each branch. I loved how they were anxious for spring to come.

I stopped in front of her stone and let my pulse slow down some. Beneath the layers of clothing, my shirt was damp. The sky approached blue as I listened to myself breathe. My fingers traced the letters of the date cancer took her away from Dad and me, just over two years ago. I don't think I'll ever be able to have a fun New Year's Eve. Next, I ran my thumb over the stone's smooth lettering. *Jenna Lender.* I mumbled my usual morning hello to her. It made me feel like we still had a connection. As long as I visited every day, that connection wouldn't fade.

The clouds cleared, and I resumed my jog back towards home. The last three blocks always set off a chain of barking dogs, but by that time most people were up. I tried to get home just before Dad left for work. He taught at a private school on the other side of the county, so his day was always longer.

Yet another morning without seeing her, whoever she was, but I had logged almost four miles. I slowed down and caught my breath by the mailbox. Dad and I had to attach it back onto its post last Halloween. We never replaced the door, and the metal was still dented on one side just below the 176. I noticed a little slip of paper peeking out. It was folded into thirds and taped shut against the inside of the box. I looked around for the female runner.

3

Nothing.

I picked the tape off the paper and unfolded it to find a message:

Mark,

Whenever you're ready for me, I'm waiting for you.

I jumped at the sound of the garage door opening. Dad's gray Civic backed out. I shoved the note under my shirt like I was hiding a Playboy and waved goodbye to him.

2

I didn't see Brian until we met second hour, because it was one of the few classes we had together. For a science class with so few labs, it always smelled like one had just taken place involving sulfur and ammonia. According to the posters draped on the walls of the Pond Bridge High room 17, the periodic table only had 111 elements, and Pluto still counted as a planet.

I sat down next to my friend at our back row table while he texted away to his girlfriend. No wonder he didn't reply to my text about showing him something. The way he squinted, along with the gray hairs that already sprouted above his ears, made Brian look much older. I remembered at least three times when we were out to eat and the waitress offered him one of the drink specials.

My backpack contained the note, so I set it on our table next to his oversized coffee mug I'd have to hear him slurp through. He still needed to copy my Spanish homework.

"I've been waiting," he said.

"Dammit, was that from you?" I'd be lonely forever.

"Was what from me?"

"You said you've been waiting. The same wording as the note." I tapped my backpack.

"What note?"

"I'll show you in a second, hold on."

The substitute teacher called out roll and fiddled with the DVD player while the class began to grumble. Brian slurped his coffee. "Well?"

"Wait until it's dark," I said.

"Hey, that's my girlfriend's motto." Josh Harding had heard me and turned around. Coupled with a large wave of blond hair, Josh's voice matched his father's tone, which all of Pond Bridge had heard a million times from his dealership's commercials. Most of the pickup trucks in the school's lot had been acquired through a sale from the infamous Bill Harding. "Getchoo a deal!" Josh was just as naturally gifted with communication, so he knew how to sweet-talk most teachers without them ever catching on. Since arriving in our district during the middle of third grade, Josh had provided volumes of entertainment while absorbing the consequences, all for the sake of humor. There were times when we couldn't tell if he was serious or joking around, because he was so gifted at false sincerity.

I waited until Josh turned back around. The lights finally clicked off. Once the film's narrator began droning on about the power of the human brain, I unzipped my backpack. The note was crumpled a bit, like the treasure maps I used to create last year when I was bored in study hall. The scribbles weren't clear enough for Brian's eyes, so I reluctantly handed it over to him to inspect.

Josh turned back around. "I heard a zipper," he said. "Sorry, just a reflex my girlfriend trained me with."

Brian held the note up like he was examining an X-ray. I tried to push his arm back down, but it only garnered more of Josh's attention.

"What the hell is this?" Brian said. His dark hair moved with his ever-growing forehead and his raised left eyebrow blew any chance of losing Josh's interest. "Who...?"

"No idea," I whispered.

"C'mon, give it here," Josh said.

"Young man," the sub said in her stern voice.

"Hi, I'm Josh. I apologize." He bowed an apology and nodded

6

his head at Brian.

"Just don't show anyone," I told Josh. I slid the paper to him, but he outdid Brian and held it up like it was show and tell. He mumbled the first part but then slid his chair back and laughed when he finished reading it.

"Whenever you're ready for me," he said even louder. Everyone turned and looked at us. "Lender, this chick wants you."

"Young man. I mean, Josh! I've asked you to stay quiet during the movie."

"I'm sorry, but my friend Mark is finally going to. . ." He folded the note back up. "I'll be quiet now." The sub opened her mouth, but as Josh put his head down she decided not to take any action.

I wanted to punch him, but of course I didn't. I never got into trouble before, and usually Josh and I got along because someone else was the butt of his antics. This time I was the target. My temperature rose a bit, and I could feel the smirks and side-eyes from my classmates.

"So did you plant this?" I asked Brian.

"Did it appear in school or was it mailed to you?"

"I found it in my mailbox, but it was just stuck there. You know what, never mind." I snatched the note back off the table and shoved it in my pocket as Josh started to turn around again. I wanted to shoot lasers through his face, but glowering isn't my specialty. Instead, I pressed my lips together to look hurt.

"Oh, don't give me that puppy-dog stare," Josh said. He was finally being discreet, so the sub pretended not to notice us. "I'm sorry. It's just a note from some chick who wants to bang you. It's not like I showed naked pics of your…"

Josh finally turned around.

I thought about the handwriting. Was it a hoax? The writing was girly, but one of their female friends could have helped. I wasn't popular enough to get hazed by the cooler crowd, so if it was fake, one of my close friends was to blame.

I trusted Brian with a lot of my personal business, meaning he had seen me cry quite a few times over the years. He was there for me when I lost Mom, but there were times he could still be a bastard. One morning in seventh grade while I was out for a dentist appointment, Brian went around telling everyone I was in love with Leah Hayden. There was no question it was him, because he sensed I always had a thing for her. By the time I got back for lunch, the whole cafeteria was teasing me. Chants started up. "Mark's in love! Run, Leah, run!" I spent the next half-hour crying in a bathroom stall. Brian still denies starting the rumor, so he's never apologized to me or Leah. Someone told me she cried that day too.

There was nothing wrong with Leah Hayden back then, and there's even less wrong with her now. The only student standing between me and becoming the runaway candidate for valedictorian, Leah seemed to be in her own little social class—aloof. She'd gotten tormented a lot in grade school and didn't forget it. The trait she caught the most crap for was that her eyes were two different colors. Blue on the right, green on the left, like two unmatched gems. They gave her an intriguing look, and I think it made other girls feel threatened. Her hair was a shade darker than red, and during the warmer months, freckles patched her face. They always seemed to favor the side with the green eye. Freckles are like vegetables. As a kid they seem awful, but at some point you grow up and think, "Hey, I could go for a salad."

The DVD ended a few minutes before the bell. If I could start the day over, I would have kept the note to myself. I could tell Brian wasn't done with the topic. He tapped his mug on the table like he was mining for wisdom.

"Maybe this will help you start a mature relationship. Love is a wonderful thing, you know."

I glared at him because it gave Josh permission to start back up, too. "Seriously, ladies in the room." Heads turned from phones. "Ask all of your friends who's after Mark here, so we can get this boy on the right path."

A few laughs pelted me from behind, and I felt the blood pulse through my cheeks. Just like the sub, I had no way to shut Josh up.

3

At lunch I scanned the tables in the distance just in front of the spirited banners our cheerleaders draped across the trophy cases. "Go Greyhounds!" was their sound advice for the varsity basketball team. I was on the JV squad, so my season had ended the prior week. Local media projected the varsity team to get slaughtered in their upcoming tournament game. I wouldn't mind seeing that happen.

As far as Pond Bridge sports went, there was only one team who gained the area's attention. From the old folks who got to Perky's at 7 a.m., to the functioning alcoholics who frequented the area bars in Elk Falls, Greyhound softball was something to talk about with pride. Championship banners sprouted from the ceiling of the gymnasium.

I hesitated before sitting down. What if the jerks at my table found out about the note? Every day insults flew like bullets, because we couldn't just sit there and eat. I had no allies, so usually I kept quiet. They often smelled weakness and fear, so I tried to give off an optimistic vibe. Maybe I could catch the eyes, or at least a clue as to who sent the note. Someone in the building, maybe even in the cafeteria at that moment, wanted me to notice her. The message was still in my front pocket, and I couldn't help but check every few minutes. I couldn't risk it hopping out of my jeans.

The biggest reason I hated our varsity team, Jefferson Reed and his short black hair, sat across from me. His long legs claimed the space where I should've been able to keep my knees. Jefferson never wore anything but gym shorts and other overpriced athletic wear at school. He liked to go sleeveless to show off the stupid tattoo of a falcon on his right arm. His eyebrows slanted down so that he always looked angry, or as most of the girls described it, like a bad boy.

I ate as much as I could before my table got too crowded. The rest of the guys who played varsity alongside Jefferson filed in. Was the daily hostility worth it? I lied to myself, believing that these guys still considered me a friend. Before high school I was one of our best players and they treated me as an equal, but somehow in the last few years I'd fallen behind physically, and therefore socially.

In previous years, I sat next to Brian and his elbows. Among our pals of a slightly less popular but friendlier crowd, we laughed, lied, argued, and forgave each other, only to do it again the following day. But this year, Brian had been elected as a student ambassador by the teachers. This bullshit honor earned him a student office privilege that he shared with the only other ambassador who'd run, Leah (who I'm sure he still hasn't apologized to, either). Basically, they were in charge of showing outside guests around the school, attending a few student conferences at other local schools, and mediating between students who had conflicts with one another. As rare as those duties were, they were given an office with computers to plan and organize during their lunches and study hall. I took my buddy's absence personally, and we argued about it often.

For Brian, the main perk of being ambassador, and the only reason he'd applied, was that ambassadors were allowed to bring a date from outside of the district to school dances. This was a must for Brian, who exclusively dated girls who didn't attend Pond Bridge. I think it's because they never forgot in third grade when he peed his pants. "I like the outsiders better," he always said.

10

Every week I begged him to come to lunch in the cafeteria, but he wouldn't. "Just eat with me in our office. Leah won't bite."

I wasn't sure about that. Plus, Brian spent most of his lunch texting his girlfriend. So instead, I did my best to fit in with the guys who used to be my height. Some days I even spoke first. Maybe a question would quell their cruelty.

"How's practice going? You get the scouting report on West Plains yet?"

"It won't matter. Our season will be over just like yours," Jefferson said. I dug around in the bottom of my brown bag, but Jefferson wasn't done with me. "Hey Mark, you think it'll be weird being the first senior to play JV next year?"

I flashed a fake smile. I'd sacrifice a whole point of my GPA to shut that asshole up.

"And in two years maybe you can come back from college on Friday nights and suit up," Jefferson said. The laughs started to bubble up. "Mark will be like sixty, still playing JV ball." He cupped his hands around his mouth. "Starting at guard, a senior...citizen. Number twenty, Old Man Lender!"

"What'll be cool is that you guys will still be season ticket holders because you'll never leave this hole of a town." Like a lot of my insults, it took them a second.

I pulled out the last item of my lunch.

"Nice lunch there, princess," Jefferson said.

I looked at the pack of Disney fruit snacks in my hand.

"My God, what grade is this?" His teammates laughed while I struggled to swallow the last one. "Be a grownup and stop packing your lunch."

I'd had this argument with Dad many times, begging him for just a couple of bucks a day instead of brown-bagging it, but he wouldn't budge. He said we were still in too much debt and that money could go towards something better. I told him to look around at the kids who packed their lunches at the school he taught at, but he said private school kids in Perry aren't people we should compare ourselves to.

11

"Here, I'll share some grownup food with you." Jefferson lined up a row of peas across the table. They were dark and mushy and had probably been in a can since we were in grade school. He cocked his index finger back and unleashed a rapid fire of vegetable pellets into my chest. One even caught me in the nose, which encouraged two more shooters to attack. I had a lap full of peas to brush onto the floor.

"Boys, don't make a mess," Mr. Mallett said while walking past. He patted Jefferson's shoulder on his way. Mallett was the new interim vice principal strictly in charge of discipline issues. I didn't know much about him except that he was born without a sense of humor or a neck.

"Pick 'em up," Jefferson said as Mallett walked out of range.

I reached down as if to obey, but brought my middle finger up instead.

"Finally a point for Lender," Andy the point guard said, slapping me on the back hard enough to film a Heimlich instructional video.

I looked back to see if it was safe to leave them there. Mallett wasn't looking, but I would find out soon that my admirer was. Then someone else approached.

"Oh, *now* what does she want?" Jefferson said. The rest of the guys turned their heads.

Angel Hayden weaved her way to our table. Since her sophomore year when she finally stopped growing, all the sports programs had her listed at 6'1" or almost a solid foot taller than her sister Leah. Angel didn't have to worry about getting bumped into in the hallways. Students stayed out of the path of her hips. She wasn't fat, but her solid frame served as a sturdy foundation for the softballs that she flamed past helpless batters every spring. Over the last few years, Angel had become the closest thing to a celebrity in Pond Bridge and the nearby counties. Unlike her sister's mix, both of her eyes were blue, and instead of freckles, her skin bronzed in the sun. Her tan added definition to her biceps and shoulders. Auburn hair didn't do it for Angel. It was probably too subtle, so she dyed it blond, but not always frequently enough to cover the dark roots.

"Fundraiser for prom, boys," she said. Her voice was hard and clear without the rasp that often accompanies a female jock.

"So they sent you to collect dollar bills. How appropriate," Jefferson said.

She palmed his head and almost yanked him out of his seat. I pumped my fist under the table.

"It's second-chance romance balloon-a-grams," she said as Jefferson rubbed his neck. "Two bucks gets you a balloon and dedication note for that special someone." She took her gum out and stuck it on Jefferson's tray where his peas previously lay.

We dodged her eye contact until Andy asked the obvious. "Shouldn't this have been a few weeks ago at Valentine's Day?"

I didn't look up. Instead, I tried to ball up every cubic inch of my brown bag so she wouldn't notice it too.

"Too many snow days." She shrugged and stood above us with a notepad and pen like a waitress forcing us to order. No one moved. "Well, if you change your mind, you know where to find me." She walked away as our eyes followed the stripes that twisted around her black and silver yoga pants. Her sales pitch began again a few tables down.

"We sure do," Jefferson said, leaning in like we were all in a huddle. "On the front lawn of a frat house." Even as he said it he glanced back in her direction. I'd drop another point in my GPA to see her beat his ass.

I got up and threw my crumpled bag away, still looking for whoever wanted me to notice her. I sipped from the water fountain and took my time returning to the table, but no one sent any signals. I was about to sit back down when Mr. Mallett appeared next to me. His nose seemed to twist on his moustache. "Forgetting something?" he asked. Black coffee breath blew in my face. I started to sit down, but he cut me off.

"Marky Lender?" His stomach almost collided with me.

"Just Mark, sir."

"Come with me." I followed him out of the cafeteria.

I listened for an explanation, but he stayed a half step ahead of me the entire way. I felt like a trespasser as he led me behind the secretary into his office. Was there some award I had won and didn't know about? I stood there certain that I had done nothing wrong, but his frown seemed to contradict that. He closed the door behind me and pointed at the only chair in front of his desk.

The room was so different from the last time I'd been in it. Its previous owner, Mr. Pierson, had been a mentor of mine, especially during the worst months of my life when Mom passed away.

We'd guessed Pierson was barely in his thirties. Everyone respected him for his work ethic and school spirit. You could even find him in the middle of the student section at the big rivalry games leading cheers for a quarter before returning to his post at the gate. His mother died when he was young too, and without his encouragement and guidance, my first two years of high school would have been even more painful. He had always been there for me.

I missed Mr. Pierson's decor of sports posters too. Without his personal touch, the office seemed to come from a different decade. Who'd have ever known there was wood paneling underneath his magnificent framed poster of Soldier Field?

Now the office was the cave of his replacement, Mr. Mallett. The right side of the small room had a stack of a half-dozen unpacked cardboard boxes. He had to squeeze by them just to get to his seat.

"Sit down, young man."

I've found that it's never a good sign when an authority figure calls you 'young man.'

"Still getting settled in?" I asked.

"It's only been a few weeks."

"May I ask why Mr. Pierson left so abruptly? No one really told us students and we always got—"

"No, you may not," he said and cleared his throat. "We're not starting any rumors."

14

I looked back over at the boxes. There definitely wasn't an award for me hiding in any of them. Mr. Mallett finally sat down and leaned back in his chair. It squealed like a wounded animal.

"Marky."

"Just Mark."

"You must not be aware of the hardworking students who help our chefs prepare lunch. Or the hardworking custodians who clean up every day."

Chefs? "I don't follow, sir."

"People make that food and clean those floors, and then a guy like you has the..."

I almost said "balls" for him, but it wouldn't have helped.

"The nerve to throw peas all over the floor."

This was going to be easy to explain! "Those were thrown *at* me, sir." My adrenaline kicked in, causing my voice to quiver.

"Oh yeah? By whom?" Again with the coffee breath.

I looked down into my lap and weighed the consequences of ratting out Jefferson versus the punishment of a first-time-in-my-entire-life offense.

"And then," his voice got louder and "then" got an extra syllable, "after I tell you to clean them up, I have a witness tell me you gave me the finger as I walked away."

A laughed slipped out because it was so absurd. "Sir"—I couldn't use that word enough—"I'm a 4.0 student with no record. I know you're new here, but I'm not dumb enough to flip off a principal, especially in a crowded cafeteria." I folded my arms. "Call Pierson up and ask him what kind of student I am. What kind of person I am." I really missed him. "Also, I packed a lunch today, so the peas *couldn't* have been mine."

He snorted. I thought back to the ethos, pathos, logos lesson we learned as freshmen when Atticus Finch used them during his closing arguments. I'd hit two out of three. Not bad.

Mallett glared straight into my eyes. I had no problem looking back. I even did my best not to glance at the stray hair under his chin. "I promise. I pack my lunch every day because we're still paying off my mom's medical bills. Cancer treatments are expensive even when they don't work." How's that for ethos?

"Hmm," is all he said before reaching into his drawer.

"Again, you can ask Mr. Pierson."

"After school detention. Tomorrow." He scribbled the sentence onto carbon paper and tore off the pink copy for me. "3:15, Friday, in room 101." He snorted to himself.

I got the allusion. "A place where there is no darkness," I said as one last chance to connect, but he didn't acknowledge my reference.

"One more thing," he said. His nostrils whistled. "There's a young lady named Katy Mancer waiting in the hallway for your apology."

"Who?"

"The eyewitness."

The tattle-tale. Leaving Mallett's den was like exiting a portal. The fluorescent lights in the office made me squint. How long was I in there?

"Will you need a late pass to your fifth hour?" the secretary asked.

"No. She knows I'm a good student," I said, looking back at Mallett as he closed his door. He pretended not to hear. I folded the detention slip and slid it into my pocket next to the note from my admirer. I thought about how different everything had been twenty-four hours ago. I needed to get to my locker before Spanish, but as promised, someone was outside looking for an apology.

"And there he is," the girl said. She adjusted her oversized glasses and pushed them up against her thick eyebrows. Curly dark hair tangled down onto her shoulders, which still held up her green apron from washing dishes. Her exaggerated frown looked drawn onto her face.

"You Katy?"

"Duh." I couldn't figure out why she was puffing so hard. Allergies?

"Well, sorry I didn't clean up the peas that everyone threw at me."

"You'd better be."

I took my focus away from her dark eyes and gazed up to the framed picture above her. The tiny faces from the class of 1996 watched on with interest but didn't offer any support. "And thanks for the detention." I thought about showing her the slip, but changed my mind. "I guess that's it."

"No, it's not." Her frown curled into a smile. It reminded me of that scene from the Grinch when he devises his plan. "I'm waiting."

Oh shit, those same words. "Well, what else do you want from me?"

She glanced up for a thought, then returned her stare. "I want your love and affection. Your body." She said it like a fast food order.

I stepped back. "Wait, what?"

"That's how you'll make it up to me." No logos there.

"Do you live in town?" I asked.

"Just a few blocks from you. It'll be perfect. We'll sneak into each other's..."

As I walked away I deflated a little more with each step. Furious, I entered the restroom where someone was vaping in the stall. I pulled both the note and the detention slip from my pocket and tore them into as many pieces as I could. Then I sprinkled them into the trash can like confetti that rained down on my parade of disappointment.

The next morning I cursed at my alarm but still got up to run. How stupid of me to think that my dream girl admirer would be an attractive fellow morning runner. Of course it was someone insane. The thermometer at the bank said 38, and the wind still swept between the gaps in the small buildings. I found myself looking around more so Katy couldn't sneak up on me, and I stayed on Main Street until I turned around at Edge Road. I was pretty sure she didn't live on Main, but she must've been somewhere near my

17

house. Her outfit had suggested she wasn't from one of the larger homes to the north.

At least I kept my streak of visiting Mom's grave intact. At her stone, I knelt down and vented my frustration and disappointment. The frost dampened the knee on my sweatpants. "You saw that the detention wasn't my fault. I'm not going to tell Dad about it either." Those few minutes with her were often the best part of the day.

4

Mr. Bates and I had the same question as we met in room 101 that afternoon. "What are you doing here?"

His answer was easier. "Getting all my post-school duties out of the way before track season. I take it you have a reasonable explanation, Mark?"

I stood in the doorway ashamed. Mr. Bates was my favorite teacher and coach. Like Mr. Pierson, I could confide in him. The two had worked together so that I was able to take calculus as a junior. He felt like one of us sometimes, with the way he stifled swear words under his breath or rolled his eyes when a kid did something really stupid. He wasn't married, and on certain days my classmates would whisper that he was hungover. I didn't trust the other teachers the way I trusted him. The bond we'd built during previous track seasons only brought us closer.

"Someone threw peas at me during lunch yesterday and I didn't clean them up," I said. "Then a scary girl saw me and told on me."

"A scary girl?"

"Katy or something. Probably a sophomore. It's okay. I can finish up that homework you accidentally assigned us on a Friday."

He laughed at my jab. "Well, if no one shows up we'll head out of here as soon as you complete it. Deal?"

I paced around the small windowless room looking for a desk that didn't have genitals drawn on it. There were only two rows of three, but the back left seat would do. Someone had carved their love for Metallica on it years ago. When I sat down, the legs screeched against a floor that hadn't been waxed in years.

"Oops, looks like we got one more," Mr. Bates said. "Speaking of scary."

The room shrank to a shoebox as Angel Hayden engulfed the doorway. She reached up and grabbed the top frame of the door. "Bates, can I make up that quiz I missed?"

"Now?"

"Yep. Get me out of softball conditioning. We're running laps, and I feel like shit."

"Angel—"

"Sorry." She looked over at me. "Didn't know anyone else was in here."

I knew I was invisible to popular girls.

Mr. Bates dug through a folder looking for a copy of the quiz. "Let me run up and get it," he said. "Mark, don't go anywhere."

The room went from a shoebox to a jewelry box. "Hey," she said. "Who're you?"

"Mark."

"Oh, Lender? Marky Lender?"

"Just Mark." It was like she was the sun and I could only make quick glances in her direction.

"Care if I sit by you?" I balked at a shrug, so she took it as a yes. Her black shorts still covered most of her thighs, but her homemade white tank top had been scissored at the sleeves.

In my peripheral vision I caught a glimpse of a bright pink sports bra hugging her side. Her Nikes tapped on the floor in the rhythm of a heartbeat. The clock on the wall ticked, but the second hand was stuck at the six, making the time an eternal three eighteen. The part of my brain that does calculus shut down. I tried not to breathe too loudly and actually started holding my breath like I was under water.

Mr. Bates returned. "Angel, you know Mark? He's pretty good at this stuff."

"Yeah, kinda. I bet he's the one from your first hour who always ruins the curves." I gulped a bit. "I prefer to show mine off," she said, sitting up straight in the undersized desk. Bates and I pretended that hadn't just happened. "I guess I'm more of a reader myself," she said. "But if you know math..." She slid her desk even closer.

She smelled like artificial fruit flavors. Was it gum or lotion?

"Careful, Mark, she's pretty clever," Mr. Bates said. Anything to put layers between her prior comment about curves.

Angel turned in her desk and faced me, inspecting. Her bare knees were almost touching my thigh.

"Today I'm giving everyone similes. Let me do Mark," she said slowly while looking up at Bates to see if he caught the joke. "What could I do with Mark?" she whispered. I envied how turtles could just duck their entire bodies inside a shell.

"So Mark, you're kinda like... like the second verse to a song." She nodded, happy with herself. "I feel like people kinda recognize you, but you don't stick out."

"Does that make you the first verse then?" Mr. Bates asked. He seemed to take more offense than I did.

"No, Bates, I'm like a chorus. I get stuck in your head, and I won't go away." The two of them laughed. I tried to laugh too, but it came out as a nervous cough.

"So can Mark help me with some of this if I get stuck?"

"Angel, it's a quiz."

"I know, but I was out sick when you reviewed."

"Fine. I'm just going to sit up here and grade, and if you can get anything out of Mark about your work, good luck." He popped the cap off his red pen.

"Nice," Angel said. "Let me work out the front page on my own."

One. Last. Problem. That's all I had left on my worksheet. Without her there, I'd be ready to go home, plop down in front of the TV, pick up the controller I charged up last night, and forget that girls even existed.

"Batesy," Angel said.

He sighed instead of answering.

"There's a lot of rocket ships drawn on my desk." He ignored her and continued slashing red lines through the paper he was grading. I thought about making a mad dash before she asked me if *I* had a rocket ship. Just one more problem.

I watched from the corner of my eye as she scribbled through the same calculus quiz I had aced earlier that week. Her desk was still angled towards mine so whenever she erased, she ended up sweeping the shavings in my direction. I listened to her whisper through the steps of solving each problem. I don't know how, but she made it sexy. Then she'd undo it by bursting into song when she thought her answer was correct. She'd occasionally tap something into her calculator and then use it as an imaginary microphone to resume her tune: "The function of f is greater than one third. I said greater than one third, greater than one third."

A few more minutes of this passed, and I finally completed my worksheet. I unzipped my backpack, placed the sheet inside, and then zipped it back up, hoping to have my release granted.

"Oops, dropped my paper," Angel said before pushing the stapled sheets off her desk. I looked down at the quiz. "That means I need help," she said softly.

By instinct, I glanced to the front of the room. Mr. Bates only shook his head and kept grading.

"Let me see," I said.

"He speaks."

"First page looks good."

"I bet you say that to all the girls you help with calculus."

"Not really." It was easier to talk if I kept my eyes on her paper.

"You mean, I'm your first? Did you hear that, Bates? I'm his first. And to think, we just met, and he hasn't even taken me out to dinner yet, and—"

"Angel, for Pete's sake, the kid is trying to help you," Mr. Bates said.

"Oh, I'm just kidding." I noticed her tugging the side of her shirt down. "I don't do that until at least the third date, maybe after a trip to Applebee's."

I stayed silent and flipped to the next page while Angel wound her finger in her hair. "Do I make you nervous, Mark?"

Pure evil.

"Sorry," she said. Her simple apology seemed genuine and I was somehow touched from one word. Inside my pulse pounded blood through my brain, which was searching for anything to say, but I was being dissolved. I looked up at Mr. Bates, a plea in my eyes.

"What do you think, Mark? Should I send her back to conditioning?"

"No! God no," she said. "Seriously, anything but four-liners."

"I hate those too," I heard myself say.

"Right? They suck," she said. "It's like, every time I get going and have to turn around, someone's in my way. I plowed over three freshman girls yesterday."

"So far your quiz looks fine," I said, handing it back to her. She went to say something, but actually stopped herself and shifted her hips in the tight desk.

"You're a junior, right?"

"Yep."

"So is my sister, Leah."

I nodded. "Yeah, she's a student ambassador with my best friend, Brian."

"Oh yes." Angel's shoulders rose up while her posture and hands became those of a choir girl. "Ambassa-tor Leah," she said in a British accent. "Ambassa-tor Le-ah and Ambassa-tor Bri-an. They must represent Pond Bridge High and save our honor."

"Brian only does it so he can bring his girlfriend to dances," I said. "He dates a girl from South Perry."

"Oh? Who?" Angel asked. She was facing me again, the final question on her quiz abandoned on her desk.

"Carissa Kelly?"

"No way, I know her!" She put her hand on my forearm and gave it a firm squeeze.

"Angel, you done with your quiz yet?" Mr. Bates said.

"We played on the same summer league team growing up," she said. "Haven't talked to that girl since middle school, but we follow each other on Twitter and stuff, but yeah, Carissa Kelly. Guess we only see each other on the field. So weird that you know her too." I glanced down at the final blank space on her quiz. "Okay, okay, I'll finish."

I'd forgotten my jacket in my locker or else I would've put it on to send a second hint to Mr. Bates. Maybe he wasn't comfortable alone in a room with her either.

Angel pressed her lips together and started working through the final problem. She whispered a formula to herself, flipped her pencil over to erase something, but then decided it had been right. Or she no longer cared. She slid her left sneaker under her chair and bounced on the ball of her foot. My eyes wandered up and down her calf muscle. There was a tiny spot she'd missed shaving to the side of her kneecap. How was this... *woman* in the same room as me? She should be signing car leases and looking over her mortgage, or whatever adults did. But the more I watched her fight to recall the next step in her equation, the less threatening she looked.

"Ta-dow," she said, slamming her pencil down. "Done." Mr. Bates looked to the ceiling and mouthed the words 'thank you.'

"I owe you one, Marky," she said.

"Just Mark."

"Right, why do I keep adding the y? Someone called you Marky earlier." She stood back up and towered over me. "It's like—"

"No time for similes, Angel. Back to conditioning you go," Mr. Bates said. He straightened his stack of papers and stood up.

I waited for my phone to get a signal and checked for the time. So much for leaving early. It was almost four o'clock, but neither Brian nor my dad had texted. Angel loped down the hall and disappeared into the gym, and Mr. Bates followed almost as quickly. If the last hour had been a video game, I would've hit the reset button and done it over. I knew I could've said something clever. "Angel, you're like... a devil?" Maybe it was best it ended when it did.

Disappointed in myself, I returned to my locker to drop off my backpack and get my jacket. The mile walk home didn't need any cargo. It was wiser to hike up the bike trail that led into town rather than explaining my detention to Dad. I knew one parent was already disappointed (even though it wasn't my fault).

From my locker I hurried back through the empty hallways. Most of the classrooms were dark and the only noise was a custodian buffing the upstairs halls along with a few faint whistles from the gym on the other side of the building. My feet started to lead me in that direction. One more glimpse of Angel in that shirt couldn't hurt.

No. I wasn't creepy.

Outside, the sun was already napping behind the clouds. The lot was mostly empty and I took one more look at my phone. I sent Brian a text asking for a ride, but he didn't respond. This was becoming normal. When we were freshmen, he was there for me within seconds. "Your mom might be gone, but you'll always have me," he wrote in a sympathy card. The occasional reflection still glazed my eyes.

Brian was lucky. He had access to a car, two parents who loved each other, and a girlfriend. Everyone else seemed to have a ride too, and they were now getting into them on the other side of the lot. I remained near the doors where the buses had picked kids up over an hour ago. No use doing the walk of shame in front of anyone. It was already easy to feel sorry for myself. As the lot began to empty, I leaned against the door wishing to blend into the dark green paint. The wind blew right through my jacket, and the hood inflated like I was a Jedi. This helped to hide my face. The parking lot became silent again, so I stepped towards the road I would cross to get to the trail.

25

"Hey!" Angel's voice called out.

I pulled the drawstrings on my hood.

"Mark. Come here. Get your ass in," she said. Even across the lot her voice was strong.

"I'm okay," I said.

"I wasn't asking. Seriously, get in."

5

Everyone knew Angel's pickup truck: a tiny baby blue S-10 that had been on this planet longer than any of us students took her everywhere. The one working headlight flickered. The driver's side door was almost complete rust. A bed without a tailgate, and a reattached front bumper that had once found its way to the pitcher's mound the previous summer. I walked closer and smelled the burning oil. A cloud of exhaust turned red against the taillights.

"Press really hard to get that door open," Angel said from her window. I pushed against the cold handle, but the door refused to budge. Angel slid across the front seat and opened it from the inside. "It's all in the thumbs. Get in."

I stepped up and sat on the frigid seat. Duct tape held its foam padding inside. I searched for a seatbelt.

"Were you going to walk all the way into town?"

"I've done it before, no big deal. It beats four-liners." *You already talked about those, stupid!*

"Too cold for that. And my windshield," she said. Only the very bottom wasn't complete fog. It sounded like she had the dashboard fan blasting, but who could tell what worked? The radio definitely didn't. "Just give it a sec to warm up and clear off."

Whenever there was too much adrenaline in my system and I didn't move, my body began shivering. This, of course, was never beneficial. It's one of those traits that defies evolution. It happened during tests. It happened during the games of poker we'd played as freshmen. The worst part was that it was hard to hide.

I searched for anything to stay as my mind filtered thoughts like a computer virus scan. Zero results.

Angel sang a tune to herself. The melody was tone perfect but subdued. She wore a gray Cincinnati Bearcats sweatshirt with the hood down, but hadn't bothered to throw pants over her shorts. A drop of sweat dangled from each of her earlobes just below small diamond stud earrings. They must've been worth more than the S-10. With the heat that radiated off of her, the windows continued to fog, which people said happened frequently in this truck.

"I live just in town, so if you're in a hurry, you can drop me off at Main and South Street." There. I'd said something.

"Aww, don't be dumb. You're not walking home like a little kid." The windshield finally cleared, yet we were still stationary in the lot. "Plus, we cut through town anyway since we live out on Edge." The engine idled with a sputter that made the truck vibrate for a few moments at a time. What was she waiting on? I stared straight ahead hoping my silent gaze would remind her that we were leaving. I put my hood down and stared at the clock on the dashboard. Five hours ahead.

"Shouldn't be much longer," she said between her sweet humming. "There she is."

I looked out to my right to see Leah glowing in her white tennis outfit, an immaculate skirt and sweatshirt. She opened the door with no problem as I slid over towards Angel. The middle seat felt frigid on my ass. Then I realized that Leah was sitting on the spot my butt had already warmed up. I bet she thought that was gross.

"Nice outfit, Country Club," Angel said. "Have enough for a team this year?"

"Just me. Maybe next year," Leah said.

"Shocker," Angel said. "All that training for nothing."

That pretty much summed up Leah's high school reputation. Her interests weren't shared by anyone else. Art club, writing club, and now tennis were all solo ventures so they never materialized. Angel, meanwhile, owned the town's spotlight.

I stifled my shivering. I had to. I was less than an inch from either of them.

Cause: The jerks at the lunch table threw peas at me.

Effect: My right leg touched the extremely attractive bare thigh of Leah Hayden.

"Hold on, kids," Angel said, shifting into first. The truck jumped a bit and accelerated out of the lot. "Watch yourself," she said, shifting into second. "It can be pretty scary for a guy riding Amish on some of these gears."

I flinched as she dropped the gear shift almost into my crotch.

"Told ya," she said. "You know how to handle a stick?"

"I don't think so," I said.

"Neither does Leah." She laughed to herself while I dealt with my sudden fever.

The truck's heater continued to blast with the stench from the ancient engine leaking through. The floor was littered with taco wrappers, socks, a softball glove, and other workout clothes. We finally got into town, her one working headlight barely showing the familiar streets.

"You can just take a left on South and I'm a few houses down," I said.

I'm not sure if it was on purpose—it probably was—but Angel turned way too quickly, sending me right up against her sister.

"Dammit, Angel," Leah said.

"Sorry," I said even though it wasn't my fault.

"Bummer," Angel said. "No right turns to get me some of that action."

Leah let out a long sigh and stared out her window, as if Pond Bridge offered amazing scenery.

I pointed to my upcoming house. "The one with 176 on the mailbox," I said. Angel pulled into our empty driveway where

Dad's car would usually be parked by now. An assortment of Nerf toys littered the yard from one of my wars with the neighbor boy. Why hadn't I cleaned those up?

"Here, it's easier to get out on my side," Angel said. She popped the emergency brake and hopped out. I slid left, unaware that my foot was dragging an article of clothing. Just when I thought my embarrassing day was over, I looked down to see a blue sports bra hooked around my right foot.

"Taking a souvenir?" Angel said, arms folded.

"Oh geez, sorry." Was I allowed to touch it and put it back?

Cause: You're the scapegoat of the lunch table.

Effect: You touch Angel Hayden's sports bra.

She reached down and snatched it from my foot. "Normally you gotta buy me a beer to get that far, sweetheart."

Nothing came out of my open mouth.

"You're just like a. . ." I braced myself for another simile while she twirled the garment. "I don't know," she said. She scrunched up her face like she was working through another calculus problem.

"Oh, well, thank you for the ride."

"Anytime." She looked at me for an extra second and then at the ground behind me. Was I supposed to do something else? I turned and picked up the Nerf gun on the way to my door.

As soon as I got inside, I texted Brian: *I rode home between the Hayden sisters!*

He wrote back: *So what?*

His response saved me the trouble of seeing if he wanted to hang out that weekend. Instead of late nights, I continued my morning runs. My streak of consecutive days I'd visited Mom's grave continued to grow. What if God made me a deal that he'd bring her back when I got to a thousand? The hard weeks of snow and ice were long gone, so I never had a reason or excuse to let her down.

Eastern winds blew the scent of cow manure and March through the town, and the sun rose a little earlier each morning. The clumps of rotten ice disappeared from the streets, and I found myself running extra loops before school. I even got up a little earlier in case I ever wanted to venture out a little farther from town. Like onto Edge Road.

Angel was indeed turning into a chorus in my head, but the truth was I just wanted a girlfriend. Someone to hold hands with and take things slowly. Part of me wanted to prove to Brian, and maybe to myself, that I wasn't a little boy anymore. Plus, I was lonely. Mom was the only one I talked to every day, and obviously that was pretty one-sided. Even Dad seemed to be busier with school and a support group he belonged to.

I envied Brian for always having someone to go to. For problems with his parents, he had his girlfriend. For problems at school, he had his parents.

The only attention I started getting was from Katy. We didn't have any classes together, but she had other resources. At least three times a day a random classmate would walk up and deliver a message.

"Um, Katy wants to know if you're dating anyone."

"Katy asked me to ask you if you wanted to study after school."

"Katy told me to tell you that you must call her tonight. Here's her number."

There's no way all of these people could have been her friends. Some of them were fairly popular girls. By the third time I got a message from the same person, I could tell they were enjoying my discomfort, so I tried to reverse things.

"Since you're such good friends with Katy," I started, "tell her I'm way too busy during the upcoming track season." This usually dampened their grins.

Katy even resorted to more than just students. On Wednesday, Mr. Bates met me at the door to his classroom. "Seems you've made quite an impression on a sophomore who was up here earlier."

"*Et tu*, Mr. Bates?" Some half-awake seniors bumped into me as I paused next to him. "Like I told everyone else, I'm busy running track. No time for her."

Mr. Bates smiled. "Is that why?"

"Well no, but it'll do, won't it?" The bell rang but I looked to him for a little advice.

"Maybe just tell her yourself."

"When?"

"At track conditioning."

"What?"

"We're inside today. Yoga and pilates."

Shit.

6

The carpet in the Pond Bridge library was the only thing in there less than five years old. Shelves of dusty books lined like dominos filled the back of the low-ceilinged room, but after moving a few tables, we had enough space to spread out on the floor. I plopped down next to Josh in the back row as Mr. Bates— who became Coach Bates after school—turned the back lights out. Instead of his slim suit-and-tie combo, he was dressed like us: gym shorts and an old t-shirt. He set up a small speaker and his phone to play a relaxing soundtrack of instrumental meditative music.

"Shoes off," he said and began leading us through stretches.

"Pssst," Josh whispered to me. "Hardly any seniors this year."

It wasn't the seniors I was worried about. With each stretch, I glanced back over to the door as if someone was going to enter with a loaded gun.

"Guess that makes us the team studs," Josh said.

"I don't think of track as a sport with studs," I said. "Maybe football, basketball and baseball, but studs don't run around in a circle with relay batons."

"Good point," he said. "Those three plus softball. That's why they're conditioning in the gym, and we're doing yoga in the library."

We began a series of leg lifts while on our backs. A few stragglers entered and positioned themselves off to the side. Coach Bates showed a little more attitude than he did in the classroom. "Take your time getting here, people. Not like it's a race. Just track. Jeez…"

The workout was over halfway done when the double doors banged open again. I figured someone else would face the wrath of classic Bates sarcasm, but this time he didn't say anything. I looked up in time to see Katy stepping over torsos and limbs to get to me. She wore blue jeans, high-top sneakers, and a stained Billy Ray Cyrus t-shirt. It wasn't her outfit that made Josh finally say something, but instead the odor that assaulted us when she took off her shoes.

"Aww, hell naw," Josh said at his usual volume.

"Oh, hi, Marky," Katy said.

I winced and moved closer to Josh, who looked like he had a lot of questions.

"Okay, everyone flip over into the plank position," Coach Bates called out. "Your body should form a straight line. Rest on those forearms and spread that weight out to your toes."

Planks were my specialty. When I was younger, Dad had me do planks instead of being spanked. At a very young age, I trained myself to do them on my own so that it would never be that bad. Josh and most of the others quivered as we hit thirty seconds.

"Wow Marky, you're like not even half trying," my admirer said, not using her library voice.

"Quit staring at his ass, Katy," Josh said. He knew her name too?

As others fell to their knees from the plank position, I continued to push through the pain by focusing on my misfortune. Of all the girls to have a crush on me, I ended up with the one who wore jeans to practice, had feet that smell like they'd been mummified for centuries, and had more courage and confidence than anyone not with the last name "Hayden" ever should.

"Joshua, I'm going to shove my size nine shoe straight up your ass if you ruin track for me."

"Go ahead and relax," Coach called out from up front. I rested on the floor.

"And what made you decide to run this year, Katy?" Josh asked. "Everyone says it's because I have a crush on somebody on the track team, and that might be true, but I'm really fast," she said. "I run up and down my street all the time, and people tell me I'm super athletic."

I rested my forehead on the floor. This girl wasn't going to go away.

"Everybody's saying that?" Josh asked. "Well, one of those things must be true, and I don't see your name in the record books, so I'm guessing it's the crush."

"Joshua! I'm going to shove this size eleven straight up you-know-where!" she yelled. The entire team, including Coach Bates, turned and looked. I slid over as far as possible, trying to deflect the stares.

"Okay then," Coach said, getting everyone's attention back. Why didn't he yell at Katy for the outburst? And how did she go from a size nine to a size eleven? "Go ahead and roll onto your side and extend your leg up and down, following my lead."

The group's attention focused back on Coach with a few gasps and grumbles at the next exercise. I gave Josh a stare, pleading for sympathy. He could control who laughed at whom in any situation, and I didn't want to be the punching bag I had been all basketball season. Track was my thing.

"The note?" he whispered.

I nodded yes, and his expression changed. The default devilish look that could produce trademark Josh moments at anyone's expense dropped from his face. It freaked me out, because I'd never seen this emotion from Josh: genuine concern. I could tell he was trying to think of something to say, but instead he looked at me like I was on a sinking ship and all he could do was stand by and watch me drown.

35

"Mark, you know that girl is insane."

"Go ahead and switch legs and we'll start on the other side," Coach ordered. I quickly adjusted and continued my leg raises in a hopeless force field. "Keep that leg straight as you lift and lower it."

I positioned myself so that my feet were down by Katy and my head was closer to Josh. I tried to stare ahead and ignore the look of terror on Josh's face.

"Katy, that's not quite correct," Coach Bates said. She was lying on her back opening and closing her legs.

"Is she giving birth?" Josh asked. "Thank God she's not wearing jorts."

Coach rushed back and directed her into the proper position. He returned to the front and continued his instructions. "Go ahead and switch sides, but make sure you're still facing me."

"Shit," I mouthed to Josh. I was afraid to look towards her. I angled away so that I couldn't see her at all, but she took advantage of this.

Her breath blew on the back of my neck. It smelled like eggs—and maybe peanut butter. "Ehh-ehhh," she moaned right into my ear.

"Did she just shit her pants?" Josh said. Our nearby teammates laughed.

I reacted as if a wasp had just landed on me. I hopped up and jogged out to the water fountain in the hallway. Coach Bates wasn't stupid, but if he was going to ignore Katy's antics, he'd have to ignore Josh's comments too.

I waited in the hallway for a bit and then peeked back in through the sliver of window by the door. Katy was on all fours looking like she was about to puke. There's no way she'd be able to join us distance runners if simple aerobics had her this winded. I returned to the workout and decided on a spot up front where it was safe. Coach Bates only smirked.

By the time our exercises ended, I'd rehearsed a hundred arguments with Katy in my head. But after we were dismissed, I sprinted to the boys' locker room and just sat there. I listened to the voices in the hallway and doors being opened and closed until I felt it was safe. Eventually I stuck my head out and didn't see anyone.

Quietly, I glided down the hall to make my ritual stop at my locker before walking home. The last place I wanted to be was the pick-up area in case she was lurking. I had to get back to the fire exit so I could make a run towards the bike path from there. I relaced my shoes, put on my sweatshirt and was about to bolt when I heard a whistle and some clapping coming from the other direction. The softball team and Angel were still training in the gym.

Maybe I'd wait a few more minutes inside just to be sure Katy's ride had picked her up. The best water fountain was right outside of the gym, so I decided to hydrate before the trek home. There was nothing wrong with that. From the dark hallway I looked into the gym, as anyone would.

The blue and green banners from yesteryear dangled from the rafters. A generation ago the giant words painted on the far side of the gym—"This is Greyhound Country"—had been more meaningful. The exception to these title droughts included the last few years of girls' volleyball, basketball, and of course softball. A good deal of that success spawned from the efforts of the owner of the blond ponytail with the longest stride in the gym.

Angel's shorts weren't as lengthy and baggy, which made her legs appear even longer. To think, I'd sat right up against them that whole ride home on Friday. One of her tube socks was pushed down to her ankle, while the one on her right leg nearly reached her knee. I couldn't decide which look I preferred. The leg with the pulled-up sock made her quadriceps look tanner, but then her bare calf on the other leg was attractive too. I thought about it a little longer and settled on the left leg.

After every sprint, she encouraged her teammates, from her fellow seniors to the tiny freshmen who were bent over in exhaustion. Odd to see her so serious with a sexy scowl across her face.

The hallway got darker and darker as the sunlight that angled through the windows disappeared in the late afternoon. Angel glanced my way and I froze. She couldn't have seen me. I was several yards back from the door and the windows weren't wide enough to see through from across the gym. But even if she did, so what? I wasn't doing anything wrong. I wasn't some enemy spy from across the county. Even Mr. Mallett couldn't do anything to me at this point. I had just been on my way out and needed the water fountain.

After another set of four-liners and wall-touches, I noticed how much sweatier Angel was than anyone else. Her light gray shirt was now dark except for a few islands of dry spots on the side. She lifted it to wipe her forehead. I imagined her in a headband, but didn't think it would work as well. She pulled the rest of the shirt up and over her head, tossing it to the wall like a wet rag. There was the same blue sports bra that had bear-trapped my foot the other day! Her abs shone in the lights as she put both hands above her head to catch her breath.

I found myself leaning against the nearest wall. I could've been halfway home by now, but what was the hurry? I was just standing in the hallway of the school I attended, minding my own business. I'd get another drink before the run home after Angel finished her wind sprints.

"Oh, there you are, Marky." Moment over.

I turned to see Katy aiming her chin up at me. She straightened her glasses and stuck out her front teeth a bit. "I'm sore from yoga, aren't you?"

"Not really," I said. It was time to talk with her before any more of the school heard about it. She scared me, but in a different way. My usual shyness seemed to evaporate every time we had an encounter. "Look, I don't know what you want, but it's just…" How could I say this to make it clear?

"My shoulders hurt. Maybe you could just rub them for me," she said and started pulling her sweatshirt off. Whether it was static, grease, or maybe even done intentionally, her t-shirt was coming off with it, so I ran. The emergency door banged open and an alarm sounded as I sprinted to the bike trail without looking back. The temperature dropped thirty degrees and my lungs burned. All the extra water I had taken in sloshed around in my stomach and my side cramped almost right away. Despite all that, I'm pretty sure I set a personal record for getting back into town on foot.

7

I explained to Coach Bates that I would do my optional conditioning on my own the rest of the week. He argued at first, but when I told him I was running three or four miles every morning before school, he relented. I promised I'd be in the best shape out of anyone when practice officially began that next week.

One morning when I was almost home from the cemetery, I felt a few sprinkles. The breeze picked up, but only from the side, like it wanted me to scoot over. I never complained about the wind when I ran. A few years ago, I was out on the porch with Mom. She had finished her rounds of chemotherapy and the doctors had moved on to radiation, so some of her hair was actually growing back. It wasn't even an inch long, but it grew in dark and thick. The days of seeing the creases in her skull were over. She stood still and closed her eyes. "I haven't felt the wind in my hair for so long," she said and began crying. Running in the wind will never bother me.

I increased my pace even though I was exhausted. The drops tapped my forehead and teased my squinting eyes. Three or four steps later, the pitter-patters morphed into sheets. The rain came down on me like nature had rehearsed the moment. Puddles emerged, and it didn't matter where my feet landed, because I was already soaked. Sometimes you just can't escape it, but at least my streak stayed intact that day.

By the first of March, mornings were mild, and even though I still ran in my sweatshirt, I couldn't see my breath anymore when I stopped for Mom. I worried about Katy following me in there some day. Would I be allowed to yell at her then? It was so creepy the way she just popped up in hallways, always acting like it was accidental. "We keep running into each other," she'd say. Fortunately, other than Brian, Josh, and the rest of the track team, no one really knew about it.

Somehow the cafeteria lacked its usual afternoon buzz for a Friday. I didn't mind the rare silence at my table. I saw Angel enter from the hallway and thought the day was getting even better. She was dressed up, and I didn't care if anyone saw me staring.

Instead of her usual ponytail, her hair was straightened and fell perfectly over her shoulders. Her blue eyes melted me. I'd never seen them with eyeliner. Lipstick brightened her mouth, and her smile popped even from the other side of the room. She wore a white, fitted button-up shirt. I decided my favorite buttons were the three at the top she had ignored. The shirt was untucked and barely covered the waistline of her tight black pants that made her legs look slim, almost like a model's. And heels! My God, it finally hit me why women wore heels, and if the answer was a solution to a calculus problem, it would be the coefficient to the tangent of her amazing ass.

She sauntered up to the mini-stage in the front of the cafeteria while another senior girl who clearly wasn't as enthused followed. The other girl carried close to two dozen red balloons in one hand and a small PA speaker in the other. She set the sound system down, and let the balloons surround her head.

Angel plugged the handheld microphone into the speaker. It pierced us with feedback, but got everyone's attention.

"Shit, sorry about that," she said, unflustered. The cafeteria laughed a bit, but still hummed with other conversations.

I was in awe.

"Attention, students," Angel began. She tweaked the volume on the speaker a little more. "Here are your balloon-a-grams from this lunch period. When your name is called, please come up and get your gift."

I glanced around the table. The guys were still stuffing food into their mouths and scanning through their phones.

"First we have from Steve to Mikaela. You'll always be special." A few people clapped as Mikaela ducked her way up to the stage for her balloon.

"Next, from Joel to Becca. You're the best thing that's ever happened to me." Again, only a few students noticed, and Angel's enthusiasm started to drain with each message.

"From Josh to Wendy. You know what's up, girl." Angel struggled to keep a straight face as my buddy escorted his underclassman chick to the stage. She looked at least two years younger, and dressed like she was five years older. "I'm romantic!" Josh yelled. As always, attention was given.

"From Bitsy to John. You're forgiven." As John came up to get his balloon, Angel said, "Wonder what you did?" which earned some laughs from my table.

"We're almost done, so bear with me for these last two," Angel said. There were still quite a few balloons left. "Next we have to Jefferson, from Jefferson. I really love myself."

Before I could even laugh, he was grabbing my shoulder. "Did you do this?"

"No," I said as the rest of the table let loose. Smiling, he waved like a talk show host and went up to retrieve his balloon.

"If I find out it was you," he said when he sat back down. Angel was smiling in a way that suggested she might claim responsibility. Oh, to have that kind of power.

"Before the final one, I'd like to point out that we raised a whopping forty-two more bucks for prom from this fundraiser." She shifted her hips. "So if you're dancing in a barn this April, you have yourselves to thank."

I laughed alone at my table. How could they not think that was hilarious?

"And finally, with a donation of fourteen dollars and seven balloons, from Katy to Marky." I covered my face. The laughter reminded me of my drenched run. There were a few sprinkles, then out of nowhere it was total submersion. "Float to me, my love," Angel said theatrically.

She flipped to the next message like they were flashcards. "I'll always take you back."

I considered crawling under the table, but Jefferson lifted me up like a parent pulling a child from a high chair. He shoved me the next few steps towards the stage. Angel continued to read each card that Katy paid for.

"You're my track hero." The laughter got louder and the whole cafeteria was now enveloped with each message. "Be mine forever," she echoed over the PA system.

I stood alone on the stage in front of a sea of camera phones. "Your place or mine?" Angel's timing was that of a comedy legend. As soon as the laughs died down, she pushed them back to a crescendo.

Mr. Mallett was in the back with an expression on this face that said, "I should probably stop this, but I won't."

"Other girls may want you, but I saw you first." This one got "oohs" and "ahhs" before an even higher level of laughter. It was like I was being destroyed in a freestyle roast. I went to take a step down, but Angel put her arm around my neck the way my uncle used to when I was little. She let go and recited another card. "Give me that body!" I tried to leave again but the other girl started handing me all of the balloons. What was I supposed to do with these albatrosses all day?

"And finally," she cleared her throat as the cafeteria got silent, "There's something really cute about you." The mob of Romans was a bit disappointed in the finale, as it wasn't nearly as aggressive. Some of them even let out an "Aww." Angel reached for the last

43

balloon to give to me, but fumbled the exchange. It rose to the ceiling, leaving the long string out of reach.

"I'll get it," Angel said. I didn't understand what the difference was. I already had seven fucking balloons to carry around for the rest of my high school career. However, Angel insisted on grabbing a chair from the nearest table, walking it back on stage and balancing herself as she reached as high as she could. Just inches away, her shirt lifted and her navel peeked at me in those few seconds. Sometimes I wish moments could be paused like a DVR.

With her incredible reach, Angel pulled the last balloon down and handed it to me. The crowd seemed to be dying down with this sweet gesture, but they were roused once more as Katy came sprinting from the lunch line.

She ran up to the stage and pulled off her glasses to stare the blond goddess down. Angel didn't seem to notice. Next, Katy moved to put her arm around me, but I used the balloons as a barrier and stepped back. At least people would see how delusional she was, and that I was innocent in all this. Again she glared at Angel, who was more concerned with tying her hair back. Casually she pulled it into a ponytail and looked in Katy's direction. "Thank you for your donation," she said. I couldn't tell how sincere she was.

Katy ran back into the kitchen, stumbling and almost falling along the way, and then disappeared for good right before the bell rang.

The roar cleared out, leaving a few un-bussed trays and scattered trash on the floor. It was the aftermath of a storm. Suddenly I was not just metaphorically alone, but the only one still in the cafeteria. For the second Friday in a row, I'd be late to Spanish. I sat on the steps with eight helium balloons, their strings strangling my index and middle fingers.

The longer I sat there, the more I decided it was just as much Angel's fault as Katy's. Katy had her reasons, and I'd concluded that she was certifiably crazy. And crazy for me. I pictured a giant wheel divided into 300 slices. Each slice had a girl's name on it who attended Pond Bridge High. It spun and spun and of out of the 300 girls, it had to land on Katy's slice. Cupid shot some little bullshit arrow at her that ricocheted off her heart and then knocked a few screws loose elsewhere.

Angel didn't have to make such a big production of it, though. Jefferson deserved his humiliation, but I didn't. I put my hands over my face and thought about Mom. Sometimes when I was in pain, it helped to think about a worse pain to make the current one seem not as bad. I could block out the world when I needed to. How long would I be teased about this? Not as long as I'd miss my mother. I rocked myself for a bit and tried to put it in perspective.

"Hey, you alright?"

I looked up at Angel and shrugged. She sat down on the same step next to me, her knees slightly higher. "Quite a scene," she said.

I lifted my hand that held all of the balloons. I was ready to stand up for myself. "For one of us," I said. I gave her a second, but my plastic dagger bounced right off.

"I mean, thanks to you, she donated fourteen more dollars towards prom."

"It isn't funny," I said. "I've had to deal with her for the last few weeks. It's all anyone says to me." *No more weakness.* "And you only made it worse."

She didn't apologize, but instead leaned against me. My heart rate doubled. Maybe I was being too hard on her. "And it was sixteen bucks, not fourteen. Remember that last balloon you had to fetch while everyone laughed their ass off even longer?" There. That was the best I could do. That drove the point home.

"That last message and balloon was from me," she said. She put her arm around my shoulder, gentler than before, and pressed her lips against the edge of my mouth and my cheek. Then she got up and walked away. I listened to her heels fade down the hall. I unwound the strings from my fingers and let the balloons all rise to the ceiling.

8

I walked home on the bike trail again that night with the echoes of the mockery still fresh in my ears. The rest of the afternoon had been hell, with constant teasing in the hallways and classrooms. As great as it had been to be kissed, no one knew what really happened once the cafeteria was empty. To try to get my mind off of it, I cooked dinner.

"Smells like spaghetti," I heard Dad say as the door opened. I was about to strain the noodles as he entered the kitchen. Between the two of us taking turns, we only knew how to make a handful of meals, but it saved money.

He set his keys down, looked through the mail. Staying quiet was the easiest way to let him know I was in a bad mood.

He whistled an old song and set a copy of *The Perry Times* down on the chair where Mom used to sit. We used to have just three wooden seats around our kitchen table in our tiny kitchen. Once she passed away, the void in her chair was brutal. Neither of us could remove it, so we brought up the fourth from down in the basement, damaged leg and all, to balance things out. Now there was barely enough room to walk.

There were still signs of her around the house. Knickknacks and recipes—most of which we'd failed to recreate—filled the drawers and little shelves around the house.

I threw a string of spaghetti against the wall. Mom had taught me that when it sticks, it's done. Dad looked tired in the eyes. His was still trying to get used to his new bifocals. His dark gray hair was showing patches of white and he didn't seem like talking much either, so I backed off my urge to pout.

"Rough day?" I asked while I pulled the noodle off the wall.

"What happened to you?" He walked over and reached his hand out to hold my chin, the same way he'd done when he'd caught me trying to shave when I was eight.

I pulled back. "Has it spread so far that even your school knows about it now?"

"Knows what?"

"I got humiliated at lunch today." I explained how I ended up with a fistful of balloons from a girl named Katy who lived dangerously close to us. He stared at me in disbelief the whole time, waiting his turn to either crack a joke or give me some fatherly advice about being nice to everyone.

"And she kissed you?"

"No! But that's what everyone kept saying behind my back or as they passed me in the hallway the whole rest of the day."

"So who *did* kiss you?" He filled his Cleveland Indians souvenir mug at the sink. The ice tray in a house of two guys was empty, go figure.

I shook my head.

"Mark, who was it?"

We didn't talk about this kind of stuff, but to be fair, this was the first time there was anything to talk about. I strained the rest of the noodles, took the sauce off the stovetop and turned everything off.

"How did you know someone even kissed me? Are kids from my school texting all these rumors to your students? See what this stupid girl's doing to me? She wrote a creepy note, she tried to

47

hump me during track, and now she's making sure that word spreads to my own dad—who teaches a half hour away, mind you—that she kissed me."

"Maybe you're missing something obvious here. When you're infatuated, you tend to overlook things."

"Dad, I promise you, I'm not infatuated with anyone, and no, I didn't overlook anything. Why do you think someone kissed me?"

He stirred the sauce with a ladle. "You've got that look."

"Look?"

"Well actually, son, there's a big lipstick mark on your face."

I raced back to the bathroom mirror. The lips were right where she'd left them. I thought about the kiss. Seeing the lipstick stain took me through it all over again—a perfect antidote to the social boo-boo I had endured.

I turned the water on and wet a washcloth, but I couldn't get myself to wipe it off just yet. At the table, Dad had served pasta and sauce to both of our plates and was reading the sports page. His head tilted back as he tried to get the hang of his new glasses.

"It's still there."

"I know. I'll have to scrub it, but I'm too hungry." Such a liar.

"So are you going to tell me?"

"Just some girl."

"Good to know. That'll make this talk a little shorter, I guess."

He went back to reading.

I laughed a little bit. "Her name is Angel." I put the first fork full of pasta in my mouth

"Hayden?"

With my mouth full, he still understood me. "How'd you know?"

"There's a huge article about her right here. She's pretty big-time. I mean, yeah, she's got a few scholarship offers." Dad lowered the paper and turned it towards me. There she was.

"I know, it probably didn't mean anything." A noodle fell off my fork and left a long orange streak down my t-shirt. "I won't get involved with her."

48

"What? Why wouldn't you? You're seventeen and she's a six-foot blonde according to this captioned picture."

"One," I said.

"Huh?"

"She's six foot one. And she hasn't dated a guy in high school since she was in eighth grade."

"Who does she date, pro athletes?"

"I don't know, college guys, I guess."

"Oh, of course. The University of Pond Bridge. The renowned Ivy League school known for its journalism, pharmacy, and swell college bros."

It was obvious where I got my sarcasm. I put my fork down. The spaghetti was undercooked.

"Maybe she doesn't date high school guys because she doesn't like all of those assholes on the basketball team." He wiped his chin. "Doesn't mean you shouldn't try and date. It's what kids do."

I blushed whenever Dad cussed around me or brought up dating. I wanted to explain that Angel was no kid, but he was too enthusiastic.

"She just felt sorry for me, Dad. Besides, I can't exactly take her out for a night on the town around here, anyway."

He took his glasses off and blinked a few times. "Mark, you know how you're always asking for a better cellphone, or money to buy your lunch at school, or a new laptop?"

"And you always tell me that money should be saved for better purposes."

"This is a better purpose." He raised his glass of tap water like it was a toast and took a drink.

* * *

It's frustrating, yet fascinating, how on most school days, I sleep right up to my alarm. However, on a Saturday with absolutely nothing to get to, I was awake just after five, ready to run.

After one loop of the town, the air was starting to feel balmy. I loved the smell of spring even though it was thick with more cow manure—the regular wind pattern. At that hour, it only took a few clouds to keep it dark outside. Main Street was empty except for the cars still parked outside the bar, and the town's three stoplights were all blinking yellow.

I stopped and took my sweatshirt off at a bench just past the gas station. It would be there when I got back. It was already damp and overdue for a wash. I had worn it most mornings for I don't know how many weeks. It was too ragged to wear to school, and they would have smelled it right away.

A block farther, a poster in the window of the travel agency drew my attention. *Spring Break!* it screamed in neon letters. More enticing was the picture of two girls in bikinis standing on either side of a guy in sunglasses. He had a contained grin, and each of their tanned bodies were mid-dance. Did those two girls know he was sleeping with both of them? Or maybe that happened at the same time? How was that okay with any of them? Wouldn't just one of those two hotties have been enough? What if one of them was attracted to me the way Katy was?

I continued running north while pondering the sexual history of the two ladies from the poster. With cleavage like that, it was impossible they were still virgins, right? That wasn't fair to judge.

A car turned a block ahead of me, and the sky began to lighten. I felt pretty strong as I approached the Pond Bridge town limits. I needed to log some extra miles to stay true to the promise I had made to Coach Bates.

But it wasn't safe to run on Edge Road.

I needed the miles, and I had already completed the town loop a couple of times. Plus, I was seventeen, and there were no cars on the road at this hour. I decided then that it was safer to run out on the back roads than around town.

A quarter-mile onto Edge Road, Mom hadn't sent any lightning bolts down, so I kept going. She had been right, though: there wasn't much of a berm past the white lines. Every time I saw roadkill—and there was plenty—I veered towards the center. It stank worse than any breeze from the farm.

I continued to praise myself for this new workout. Ethos, pathos, and logos were all taking turns arguing with an opposition that didn't even exist. After at least two miles, I started to tire, and I still had all that distance just to get back home. Part of me said to keep running, because I knew what I was looking for. The other part mentioned a little common sense and asked me how it would look if I was jogging past the Hayden residence before sunrise.

The painted lines on the country road disappeared, and only a small ditch and an electric fence separated me from a herd of cattle. I had them to thank for the daily stench. They were brown and white, and their giant eyeballs seemed to follow me.

"What would you do?" I called out to them. They just stared, chewing their cud and wondering why some idiot boy was yelling at them. All but one, a calf, was lying down.

I looked up to the sky and felt it in the air. They were right. When cows lie down in the field it means that it's going to rain. It's just something us people in farm towns know about. I didn't want to get soaked for the second time in a week, so the decision was easy. I must have run over seven miles by the time I got back into town. The sky opened up as I dashed through the alleys of the final few blocks.

Dad was sitting on the couch in his bathrobe, sipping coffee and reading the paper. He didn't say anything about my odd dedication, just "I'm going to be out and about today."

I ended up spending most of the day working on a research paper that wasn't due for two more weeks. I had taken all of my notes, and after our laptop went through its half-hour startup, I began typing and editing everything until it was perfect.

When Dad got home that evening, we shared a pizza and watched basketball without him bringing up Angel. It was one of the more boring Saturday nights I'd had, which now that I think about it, was probably Dad's way of encouraging me to get a life and date someone.

That night I lay in bed trying to calculate how much farther out Angel's house was. We'd driven past it in previous years while taking the back way to Elk Falls, but I never imagined exploring the route on foot.

A little after midnight, I found my eyes starting to close on their own. My legs were already sore from overdoing it that morning. I listened to the water gush through the spouting down to the drain just outside my window. It had rained all day.

My eyes shot open. I'd forgotten to visit Mom's grave today. She wasn't going to throw lightning at me for disobeying her and running on Edge Road.

Instead, she was crying.

9

Katy was leaning on my locker Monday morning. She smiled like she had a hand-delivered bomb to ruin my week before it even started. Next to her was a boy who I guessed was a freshman. Along with being short, it looked like he had traded in every other aspect of puberty, and possibly his soul, just so he could grow a thin mustache. It looked like a prop between his smooth pre-acne cheeks.

"Excuse me," I said, trying to get to my locker.

Katy started laughing and put her hand on the boy's shoulder. I hung my jacket up and pulled out my calculus book before she finally turned to me.

"Oh no, Marky. It's not what it looks like." She put her hand over her mouth, which I wish she'd get in the habit of doing more often. Her other hand went over her heart, covering the howling wolf on her t-shirt.

I shut my locker and started up the steps, but she continued to plead. "I can explain, Marky!" People were starting to look at her.

At the top of the steps, I could still hear her feet stomping behind me. She cut me off right before I reached Mr. Bates's room.

"Marky, he's just a friend." Her breath suggested the winds were blowing in from the east.

"I don't care," I said. A classmate squeezed behind her to get by.

"Oh, I knew this would happen." Another senior turned sideways and cut right between us. "He's so upset now," she told him.

"Leave me alone," I said louder and finally bumped through the threshold and over to my desk.

She followed me in. Mr. Bates and almost everyone else paused their morning phone scans and looked up.

"He's just a friend, okay?" she huffed. "I would never cheat on you and you know that. I mean, we've been through too much to just give it all up."

"What planet are you from?" My classmates laughed.

"I hate it when he gets like this," she said to the rest of the class. The bell rang, but Katy didn't seem to notice it. "We're always fighting like an old married couple, I swear."

Mr. Bates stood up. "Katy, go to class."

She took a few steps towards the door and then faced me again. In a lower voice she said, "Marky, we can get counseling. I'll set it up." At last she left as I glued my forehead to my desk.

"You alright, Lender?" a guy from the back called out. I held out a thumbs-up.

Other murmurs continued as Mr. Bates began writing on the whiteboard. "That chick's asked me about him like four times," I heard a girl say. It was encouraging to hear that the general public was finally understanding my struggle.

Eventually I raised my head and took notes. When Mr. Bates accidentally called me Marky instead of Mark, I decided I would boycott class participation the rest of the week.

* * *

When I got to lunch late my table was silent. Subdued, they sat looking at their phones while mechanically shoveling in mashed potatoes from their trays.

"I don't see it," someone said. Whatever they were searching for kept them from noticing me and my packed lunch. I'd substituted my fruit snacks with grapes, but still felt dumb eating them.

"Here it is, just posted," Jefferson said.

Anytime there's a chance for a community laugh that isn't at my expense, I feel relieved. It reminded me of junior high when we were all the same size and got along. There were times I'd even gone over to Jefferson's house before his parents got divorced in sixth grade.

I stood up a little to see as everyone started to crowd around. He actually turned the phone towards me to get the first view. *I'm fitting in again!*

It was a picture of me. I was turned sideways with the look of a kid ready to tear into his presents on Christmas. In the photo, my mouth was open. My hands were half up like I was ready to shake my fists with joy. My eyes screamed a thousand words of pleasure as they stared at Angel's exposed stomach while she reached for that last balloon. The caption at the bottom of the picture read, "When he respects them abs!"

"Congrats, Lender, you're a meme," Jefferson said. The rest of the guys were still trying to find it on their phones. "It's on Angel's Twitter. She just posted it like ten seconds ago."

They all found it as Jefferson recapped the situation to me. "Okay, so starting yesterday her posts are 'I'm craving tacos,' then around midnight she writes, 'Can I just marry a taco?' and then today, 'When he respects them abs!'"

I wasn't even on Twitter. My crap phone didn't have enough memory and we didn't get Wi-Fi at home unless our neighbor's came into range. Dad's data allowance for me was next to nothing.

I was embarrassed, but part of me was kind of proud. Which should I have been? Angel must have been thinking about me again. I'm not thrilled that some asshole took the picture and sent it to her, but maybe it's her way of getting my attention.

The guys continued to laugh and talk about all of the other captions they could write for this picture. For once, I sat there unfazed. I had been laughed at so many times, what was the difference? Maybe I could act mad at her again. Last time that worked out pretty well.

A hand tapped me on the shoulder. I turned around to see tangled hair and glasses holding something. "Marky, here are some cookies for you." Katy set down a plate of a few intact chocolate chip cookies surrounded by a pile of crumbled ones. Her eyebrows jumped—a tell for crazy. The table of lions dropped the old scraps of my humility that they'd been chewing on and locked in on the new fresh kill of a situation.

"Go ahead, eat up," she said.

Jefferson raised an eyebrow. There was no way I was touching them. As nutty as she acted that morning, it had to be a trap.

"These took a lot of effort, Marky!" The table stifled their laughter and leaned in.

"Is there a problem here? Again?" Mr. Mallett stood behind me as well. My whole body started to hurt from being twisted for so long.

"I made Marky these cookies, and now he won't eat them."

"Marky."

"Just Mark, sir."

"Whatever, kid. Look, a woman has made you cookies in foods class. I say just eat 'em." His jiggling stomach thought it was funny. "If I see any more messes, this whole table will be spending a week in detention."

The smiles faded. "I'm taking one," Jefferson said. He grabbed an intact cookie and bit into it. The others followed his example as Mr. Mallett walked away. Only a pile of crumbs remained.

"Guess they're all gone," I said, taking the plate to the trash can. Katy stomped away. I was about to explain to everyone how they should probably have their stomachs pumped, but as soon as I sat down, Jefferson pounded the table with a fist. He lifted his hand and pointed at me. "You're banned. Tomorrow you find a new place to sit."

Everyone else could tell he was serious because the joking stopped. A few of them changed the subject, and I was too scared to look up. They would see the tears in my eyes.

That afternoon, at the end of our first official track practice, Coach Bates pulled me aside. "Mark, you're running like a madman," he said.

"I am mad," I said. Then I walked away.

* * *

By Tuesday, most of the school had seen the meme. How did I know? Brian told me it got 234 likes and 78 retweets. It must not have reached Katy, because if it had, she would have served me some sort of imaginary divorce papers in the middle of class. During science, I vented to Brian how I couldn't even take a piss without someone next to me asking me, "How's Katy?" and then laughing at my scowl.

As usual, I answered all of the review questions while Brian casually paraphrased my words onto his own sheet. Teachers called this cheating, but Brian called it gas money. The whole time he tried to tell me I should be happy with the attention.

"I guess I got Angel's attention," I said. He still didn't know how much.

"Well that doesn't count."

"Why not?"

"I mean, you're probably getting other girls' attention."

"Why doesn't it count from Angel?"

"She's not going to be into you." He squinted at my paper. "What's that word on number four?"

"Thorax," I said. "Go on."

"She's just," his forehead wrinkled, "a little too experienced, we'll say."

"What do you mean?" I knew what he meant.

"Like that praying mantis on the DVD the other day, post-coital."

"Huh?"

"After making love," Brian said.

57

"Bugs don't make love," I said. Josh turned around, but he stayed quiet.

"And neither does Angel. And she can bite the head off of a male." That wasn't the conclusion I wanted to hear, but Josh nodded along.

"Well how do I get rid of Katy?" I asked.

"A hitman will run you about twenty grand," Josh said. A table of girls two rows ahead turned around. "I'm kidding everyone, I'm kidding. Maybe fifteen."

"Bell's about to ring," Brian said. He snatched my sheet of answers and put it in his folder.

"I need that back."

"The answers to your questions and these answers will both be in my office during lunch," he said. His smile suggested it was a trap.

It was.

* * *

I went to lunch and hoped Jefferson forgot that he'd banished me from the table. I got there late because I was digging through Brian's locker trying to recover my paper. No luck.

Though my pulse was in fight-or-flight mode, I tried to look calm when I set my little brown bag onto the table. Their voices sounded upbeat. Most of the guys were chatting away and showing the usual crude jokes from the internet on their phones. Before I could sit down, Jefferson took a swipe and knocked my lunch onto the floor. I bent down to get it as if it were an accident and set it back on the table. From under the table he kicked my chair into me. It smashed my shin and toppled over. The loud slam got everyone's attention. Guys I'd been teammates with since fifth grade. Guys who'd brought home championship trophies with me in seventh and eighth grade. Guys who attended my mother's funeral and let me cry on their shoulder—they all sat there motionless.

Was I a cancer to their popularity? Did they second my exile?

I set my lunch down again and stared at him. This time he sent his fist into the bag and sent it flying past me. My apple rolled across the floor and stopped just under the trophy case. Other contents spilled out. All my little brown bag was missing was a chalk outline.

My emotions only had a few seconds left. "Fuck you," I said and walked toward the hallway leaving the crime scene for someone else to tend to.

I wasn't sure where I was going, but my composure was already there.

"Well, I've got a question," Mr. Mallett said, extending his arm in front of me. His brown and blue suit combination wasn't even close to matching.

"So do I," I said. We seemed to be the same height. "Why would a girl who wants to tell on me one week try and make me eat her cookies the next?" He frowned at my riddle. I took another step past him as he turned. "And why is my lunch all over the floor today?"

Mallett looked over to our area and absorbed the scene. I walked to the farthest restroom several hallways past my locker and stared at the mirror until the tears disappeared.

Brian's invitation. What was left to lose? I practiced my happy face, but the best I could do was my today-sucks-but-I-will-be-okay face and walked up to the second floor.

"*Student Ambassadors*" was taped on the door of room 220B. The door was cracked open, but I knocked anyway and stuck my head in.

"Come in," said a lighter voice. It was familiar though rarely heard.

"Oh, sorry. I was looking for Brian."

Leah Hayden didn't take her eyes from her monitor. Without even pausing her typing, she said, "He told me he'd be right back. Have a seat."

That jerk! I walked in like a cat unsure of its new surroundings. The office wasn't much bigger than an equipment closet. Even Mr. Mallett's had more space.

The walls were covered with archived homecoming and prom posters as well as a few out-of-date calendars with black and white sports photos. Each ambassador had a desk that faced away from one another. Brian's desk was to the right and his computer screen had gone black. His desktop had two empty soda bottles, an open bag of chips, and our science homework, all of this on top of a desk calendar that was still stuck on December. Brown rings from his coffee mugs stained the only open spaces.

I glanced to Leah's side as she continued to type. It was probably the history paper I had finished on Saturday. A stapler, some Post-Its, and a paperweight with a small piece of pink coral sat in a row to the right of her workspace.

A green candle held a tiny flame to combat the stench of Brian's salt and vinegar chips. It was one of those indistinguishable scents like cucumber and kiwi, but I was grateful. It made the office slightly more welcoming.

I sat in Brian's chair and looked over my homework. I still needed to answer the last question, so I thought I would work on it in the meantime. Where the hell was he? Even in Brian's seat, I still felt like an intruder.

Our chairs stayed back to back as I listened to her type at the speed of a professional secretary. My stomach growled a bit just as the clicking stopped.

"So, Brian said you need some help with something." I heard her chair turn, so I slowly twisted mine to face her.

Her legs were crossed in a light gray pencil skirt that matched her necklace. She leaned back a bit, but then decided to sit upright like she was conducting an interview. A high heel bumped against her foot as she straightened it every few seconds.

One look in her eyes and I was dazed. The tiny candle somehow added to their mysticism. I focused on the blue one as I tried to decide on which problem to tell her about. Jefferson? Her sister? Obviously Katy.

I looked down at my fiddling hands. "There's this sophomore." My words bottlenecked as they left my mouth. When was the last time I had actually talked to her? Sixth grade? Or maybe seventh? It had to be before the big Brian rumor incident. "Her name is Katy, and she's just. . ."

Leah leaned in to get a closer look at my squirming. My words came out like a sneeze. "How do you shoot someone down?"

"What do you mean?" She shifted and tapped a pen against her mouth. "Like if someone asks me out and I'm not interested? I guess I would just say no." She looked down like she had forgotten something. "No one ever does, though."

"Okay, so then they usually take the hint, right?" I said. I dared myself to make eye contact again. This time I would look at the green one.

"Well it's not a hint, Mark. It's an answer."

Hearing her say my name injected a bit more confidence. "Well, this Katy girl, she hasn't even asked me out. She's done all these crazy or creepy things and now the entire school is teasing me about it."

"I haven't teased you about it," Leah said.

"Well no, but you know, pretty much everyone else has." Everything I said made me feel more and more childish. Was I whining?

"I know who Katy is. She's in my foods class first hour. She's not always. . ." There was no polite way for Leah to say what I already knew.

"So what should I do?"

She shifted in her chair, keeping her eyes on me the whole time. "I've found that it's just a lack of communication that causes problems, no matter what the situation is. If someone likes someone, they don't always make it *évident* when they should. If

61

someone's not interested, they don't make that *évident* either. Make sense?"

"Wait, what was that word? Evi-what?"

"In French, *évident* means obvious or just evident."

"So I have to make it évident to her that I'm not interested." I tried to mimic her polished French accent.

"Yes, but without being a jerk about it of course," she added. "In English, not French." The smile was too much for me. I caught myself looking at a spot on the floor. How many other girls in this school had this kind of insight?

"You're really good at this stuff," I said. "So, the phrase again? If someone doesn't like someone, they have to make it—"

"Okay, from the top, in English, because the whole thing is important," she said with a calm laugh. "What causes problems in high school is ambiguity because people are scared. They're either scared to show that they like someone or scared to be honest when they don't."

I'd look up the word ambiguity later. I didn't listen very well. Instead, I thought about how not to screw up and say something dumb.

She kept going. "But hey, we're teenagers and we're all insecure, so we all usually hold back our true feelings, no matter how strong they are."

It was silent for a moment. "Except Katy," I said.

"Yes, she seems better at displaying her true intentions, better than I ever could," Leah said.

The door cracked open and Brian entered.

"What'd I miss?" he asked. I had no problem staring him in his stupid face. He had probably been on the other side of the door for a few minutes.

"Just some helpful advice," I said, getting up. "I just have to make it évident somehow." I waved my hand out like a stereotypical European.

"When you figure everything out, let me know," Leah said.

Halfway down the hall I realized I had forgotten to thank her. I would've felt stupid going back, so I texted Brian to pass my thanks along. A moment later he replied with her number.

You should tell her yourself.

God, I hated him sometimes. At least I'd stolen my homework back. My stomach let out a loud growl as the bell rang to end lunch.

10

Brian and I had somewhat of a fight that night through text messaging. He was mad at me for taking my own homework back, and I was mad at him for leaving me in there with Leah for so long. He then went on to accuse me of being afraid of girls, which led me to attacking him about spending less time with me because he was so wrapped up with his girlfriend. The whole thing would've probably been a five-minute conversation over the phone, because as best friends, that's usually all it ever took us to resolve our differences. Instead we spent two hours texting about it. We compromised on hanging out Saturday night, but with his girlfriend, Carissa, along as well. I don't think either one of us was happy with this decision of me being a third wheel, but there's no emoji for that yet—at least not on my crappy phone.

On a positive note, I found a better table at lunch. Josh welcomed me as a new audience member to his table in the far corner. On the first day we spotted Katy scanning the cafeteria for me. She took one look at Josh and his band of misfits, some of them even waving her over, and walked back into the kitchen area.

"You're like the antidote," I said.

"She knows better than to come over here with a hairnet," Josh said. Every day he presented new hilarious stories about childhood fights he got into, or his father's crazy parties with CEOs who couldn't handle their liquor. We'd laugh so loud that Mr. Mallett would feel obliged to calm us down. Josh would transform into the perfect gentleman and have Mr. Mallett chuckling on his way.

Thursday afternoon at track practice, Josh and I were running our two warm-up laps. We let Katy get just close enough before we bolted ahead. The sun was out, but the wind blew in our faces on the backstretch. The chicken fertilizer from the nearby fields stung our noses.

"Heard you really pissed Brian off today," Josh said.

"What did I do?" I knew what I did and I was proud of it.

"Today's bio test." He checked behind us to make sure Katy wasn't any closer.

"What about it?"

"Maaark?"

"Maybe I didn't quite leave my answer sheet hanging out far enough."

"C'mon Mark."

"And then I erased and switched the three answers I did show him after he turned his in."

"Ha! Nice one." He glanced over his shoulder again. "Think he'll get even?"

"What's he going to do? Tell on me for not letting him cheat?"

"Good point, but I'd keep an eye on him." Josh began a story about the time his dad peed off their balcony and the wind blew it back onto his pants.

* * *

I thought our tiff had passed, but Brian didn't say much to me during Friday's class as our teacher went over the correct answers for the test. I had aced it; Brian pulled a D-plus. He let out a lot of heavy sighs while I had no trouble showing him my paper anymore. If he cared so much about his grade, he could've done his own homework or maybe looked into that new thing the teachers are always talking about called studying.

I still found plenty of time to hit the books despite my a.m. jogs and afternoon track practices. I decided to shorten my morning runs and as a result had started another streak of visits to Mom's grave. Brian hadn't played a sport since freshman football, so I had no sympathy for him. He didn't have to cook dinner every other night or take care of his own laundry either. The louder he sighed, the more my resentment swelled.

"Still on for tomorrow?" he mumbled. Our teacher was spouting out how only three people in the class properly labeled the thorax.

"I guess. What time?"

"We'll pick you up between six and eight."

Josh leaned back. "What are you, the cable company?"

I made a face telling him to turn around. Brian crumbled up his test and threw it in the trash.

* * *

On Saturday night the sun set early, but left us with the gift of warm spring air. My ride still hadn't shown by seven, and I found myself in a backyard wiffle ball game with my ten-year-old neighbor buddy, Willie. He was an only child too, so he didn't mind chasing the balls I blasted to the next block. We turned all of the outdoor lighting on from our homes to give our adjacent yards a stadium feel.

Several innings later, I was sweating through my gray polo shirt. My legs were damp with sweat, but at least my jeans still looked clean on the outside. It was a few minutes after eight, and I wondered if I was being stood up. I could hear Brian making up some excuse about being grounded from his low test grade.

Willie was called home by his mother, but I helped him negotiate another fifteen minutes so we could clean up the front yard from our earlier Nerf gun war. Instead, it turned into another shootout.

Finally, headlights appeared and the horn honked. Brian hopped out and opened the door behind his passenger seat. "M'lady's brand new ride."

"Is that a Toyota?" Willie said, still holding his gun.

Carissa stepped out and waved. "Oh, he's adorable," she said. "Hi. What's your name, lil' guy?" She gave him a second wave, but he sprinted back behind the house. Maybe it was the dull street light, but Carissa wasn't that attractive in my opinion. Her chin was round and swollen. Her hair was a bland sort of light brown or dark yellow, I guess—not even a definite color. Her arms weren't toned like Angel's. For someone who Brian described as having "the greatest bosoms of all time" I just didn't see it. She certainly wasn't as tall as Angel either; well under six feet. I guess you could say she was stout and on the huskier side. There seemed to be a southern drawl in her words as well. Not the adorable southern belle type of accent, but instead the kind you hear from people who still phone in requests to FM radio stations.

Earlier in the evening I had asked Dad if Carissa was a well-known softball player, but he had never heard of her. She probably lacked in her simile game too.

I climbed in and was struck by the new car scent as Carissa asked where the cute little boy went.

"Oh, he's just scared of girls," Brian said. "I wonder who taught him that?" He turned around with a smirk.

"What's the plan?" I asked.

"According to Twitter, it's buy-one-get-one-free cones over at Elk Falls. It's opening night at Frosted Antlers," Brian said.

"Still not comfortable with that name," Carissa said. She shifted into drive and we jerked out of our driveway.

"Lots of people we know are over there." Brian sounded too friendly.

I frowned at him instead of asking who.

"Don't worry, Mark, we'll make sure you're not a lonely third wheel." He reached for the radio, but then decided to leave it off.

Carissa kept looking back at me in her rearview mirror. "Wait, you're the guy from that meme," she said.

"Mark thinks he has a shot with her," Brain said.

"Hayden?" Carissa said. "Love that chica. We played summer league ball together in middle school. I pitch against her soon, too, I think."

"There's another girl who's madly in love with Mark," Brian said.

Carissa looked over at Brian. They had some sort of couples' ESP going on. We all leaned forward as she braked at a yellow light.

"Gee, I wonder if she is out on the prowl tonight too," Brian said. He put his index finger on his chin.

I sat with my arms folded. I would've been better off hanging out with the ten-year-old.

"Lots of people are out and about tonight," Carissa said. She started turning down random alleys. What had I done to her? Was it the goal of every couple to humiliate those who were still single?

We circled the town twice. In a matter of hours, I'd be waking up and running this same route in silence. I didn't feel comfortable in the car anymore. Carissa's driving ability was still very green. Her foot knew no subtleties with the pedals.

"I'd better stop for gas," she said. There was still over half a tank, but we pulled into the Gasmart anyway. Carissa got out to pump while Brian skimmed through Twitter on his phone.

"She's really proud of her new car," he said. "She'll probably refuel again when we get back to her town later on."

I nodded and pretended there was something to check on my phone. It only took a minute to fill up and Carissa was getting back in when Brian yelled, "She's been waiting!"

Coming out of the Gasmart, Katy was twirling her hair. "Okay, let's go," I said.

"Wait, that's the girl?" Carissa said, lowering her window. The power locks clicked as Brian laughed.

"Please don't," I said.

"Katy, you need a ride?" Brian called out. She squinted through her glasses and walked over. "We're just cruising around with Marky, if you wanna join."

"Very funny," I said. I thought if I pretended it was such an outlandish idea instead of panicking, Carissa might not follow through.

"I gotta meet this chick," she said. "I've heard stories."

I tried to open the door but it stayed locked. "Child safety," Brian sang. He hopped out of the front and signaled Katy in. "Just climb in back," he told her. Suddenly my backseat of solitude was intruded on by a mess of hair. Her glasses fell into my lap as she crawled back head-first.

"Watch the interior," Carissa said. She finally seemed concerned, for the car at least. Katy rolled into the seat behind Carissa and reached for her glasses. I handed them to her as she tried to grab my hand.

Instead of saying hello, she just stared ahead. Brian got back in and turned to her. "Normally you'd need to buckle up, but hey, anything goes in the backseat tonight, right, Katy?"

I actually tried to get lasers to shoot out of my eyes into his face. Why was he doing this?

"Shall we get ice cream?" Carissa said.

"I have six nephews and nieces," Katy blurted out.

"Oh. That's—nice?" Carissa said. I could see her expression in the rearview.

Brian took a long look at me, then back at Katy. "Katy, do you know where babies come from?" he asked.

"Duh, Brian, I know everything about that," she said. "My sister has had six. I can even tell if it's going to be a boy or a girl."

"Oh really? How?" Carissa said.

"Even in the first trimester, I can tell by the belly," she said.

Brian couldn't wait to ask the next question, "If you had to make a baby wi—"

"Okay, Brian," Carissa said and smacked him on the shoulder. "So I head back down Main and take a right on Bridge Road to get to Elk Falls?"

Bridge Road was mostly hills and didn't even have a bridge. As soon as we left the Pond Bridge limits, we were surrounded by darkness. Carissa turned her high beams on as I considered that it would only be about a seven-mile jog home from Elk Falls. Each one of the hills were monstrous, and there wasn't much of a curb for safety. Still, I couldn't risk being seen in the backseat with Katy. "Josh Harding lives up on that hill," Brian said. "Lots of parties happen there."

Katy snorted at the mention of Josh. Maybe he could be my new best friend. The Harding fortress was with lights that beamed from the ground. They even had one of those driveways that looped around in the front.

"Oh, Katy, Brian never introduced us. I'm Carissa, Brian's girlfriend."

"Nice to meet you," she said. "I'm Katy, Marky's girlfriend."

"Oh, you two made it official?" Brian said. "I wasn't aware."

"We are definitely not a couple." It was worth breaking my silence for.

"Well, we're on a date, aren't we?" Katy said.

"She's got a point," Brian said.

I wondered if Brian would feel like it was his fault if I got hit by a car on my jog home. Maybe he'd actually apologize for once, and finally admit to the rumor he'd started in seventh grade.

"He'll come around," Katy said, sliding her hand to the small area on the seat between us.

Maybe a head-on collision would end it quicker.

Carissa jabbed at Brian's shoulder again, so he finally faced forward and pulled his phone back out. "Oh this is perfect!" he said. "Someone's dying for ice cream." We waited for him to expand, but he didn't. They left the radio off to relish the silence from the backseat.

We coasted into the village of Elk Falls. Sure enough, the familiar little yellow sign out front of The Frosted Antlers advertised "Buy One, Get One Free!" I knew Brian was brainstorming a joke about that too. I didn't even bring any money. I had declined Dad's charity so that he didn't think it was a date and ask me a hundred more questions.

The lot was half-full as Carissa double-parked off to the side. The locks clicked, which felt more like shackles, and we got out. I spread my legs a bit to stretch them. I'd never run in jeans and a polo, but I was wearing last year's track shoes, so they would suffice. No one would see me anyway. The stars were out, and Elk Falls offered little light pollution, even with the yellow lamp in the parking lot.

"I really have to pee," Carissa said, running in before all of us.

"You guys go ahead, I need to call my dad and let him know when I'll be home," I said. Maybe I could coordinate a place for him to pick me up from.

"I'll wait on you," Katy said. "How's he been? Tell him I said hi. Oh, and that it's okay to move your curfew back a few hours."

Brian bent with laughter. I waited until he'd disappeared inside before stretching a little more. Brian propped the door back open. "You should get in here," he said. Katy stood between us.

I couldn't see inside, and my trust level was at zero with him. I took a few steps to begin my trek home, and then I saw the rusted blue truck with a missing tailgate on the other side of the shop. I changed directions and walked a few paces towards the building as Katy reached her arm out in anticipation.

Right then, Angel exited the door Brian was still holding open. Her face was made up a little more than usual, and her hair was pulled into a loose ponytail. She wore tight denim shorts and a plain blue shirt that hugged her first-team, all-state frame. Her focus was on a vanilla cone with sprinkles. It seemed to have her off-balance as Brian came back out to watch the show.

She looked right over Katy at me. "Mark? What are you doing here?" I couldn't believe she'd seen me from so far away.

"Oh, just out with some friends, kinda," I said.

"Hey, was that Carissa with Brian?"

"Yeah, she just got a new car so I was riding along, but then—"

Katy positioned herself directly between us, and I can't exactly explain what happened next. Angel, true to her name, seemed to pass right *through* Katy, like she was only a hologram. I don't know how there wasn't a collision. Katy was fussing and even said, "Stay away from him," but it's like her voice was in a frequency that Angel's ears didn't pick up.

She was so oblivious to Katy, and it was one of the most fascinating things I've ever seen. Angel stopped right in front of me, holding her cone sideways and taking big licks. She rose up on her toes once or twice and then smiled.

I took a step back so that she didn't feel taller. Or I didn't feel shorter. "You gotta help me," I said.

She took another lick of her ice cream. It dribbled on her chin. "Wait, what?" She laughed again. "I was dying for ice cream. So glad this place is finally open again." She started to walk towards her truck, so I followed alongside.

"Marky Lender, you come back this instant!" The shouting became distant. Luckily Katy didn't know my middle name or she would've been scolding me like my mother did when I was a child.

The second miracle of the night was the way I was able to stay calm during my escape. "So what are you up to tonight?"

"Oh, you wanna hang out?" she asked, but I was already getting into her truck. "You gotta use both thumbs," she said.

"I know." I didn't even struggle with it this time.

She started the truck, and the engine gave a grinding roar. She backed out onto the street while taking another lick of vanilla.

"Oops, careful," I said. A car swerved around her as she shifted into first. The ice cream got more attention than the road.

"Shit, this is messy. I can't drive stick with this thing. Can you hold it for a second?"

I grabbed the dripping cone from her hand. My thumb was glazed by the time we got up to speed.

"So. Where should we go?"

"I guess back towards Pond Bridge," I said. I lifted the cone, but she was actually zeroed in on the road, her face almost directly above the steering wheel. My phone buzzed in my pocket. I wasn't even going to acknowledge it. I scrambled for something to say, but maybe the silence wasn't that uncomfortable. After a few minutes I worried about being boring. "Thanks again for getting me away from that girl. She's really. . ."

"Let's check on the field conditions," she said. "It's been so flooded lately." The soggy cone was starting to leak from the bottom, but I didn't say anything. Her driving was more important. We coasted into the high school lot and back towards the softball field before she finally let the truck idle for a moment. A burnt, oily smell surrounded us. I kept seeing signs I'd never noticed before that said: *Pond Bridge School District Property. No Trespassing. Violators Will Be Prosecuted!* Someone went to the trouble to include an exclamation point.

Mr. Mallett's office was one thing, but I didn't want to be prosecuted at the police station. They'd accuse us of trespassing, vandalism, and who knows what else. The rumors would fly, and Dad would finally ground me after assigning hours and hours of planks.

"You think the grass is dry?" she asked.

I could've just played ball with Willie all night. My phone vibrated again. "It was dry at my house, but I'm not sure it is here," I said.

She put the truck back into first gear and drove us to the right corner of the field where there was a gap in the fencing. "Angel, how close are we getting?" My laugh didn't hide my nerves. At least it was a much shorter run home from here.

"I just want to see how the field is," she said before turning off the headlights. We rolled onto the grass and into the outfield. "Gotta be careful—"

"Not to get caught?"

"To leave any tire marks. They'd kill me if I hurt the grass."

"Wouldn't they kill you just for driving on it?"

She exhaled a laugh. "I come out here all the time. Helps me prep for the upcoming games. It's my field now."

I looked behind us one more time. Maybe when you're that good, they let you do whatever you want. I was allowed to roam the halls without a pass, or just nod to a teacher when I got to class after the bell. "Did you want your ice cream back?"

"Huh? Oh sorry," she said as I handed it to her. She took one more giant bite; the cone crunched in her mouth. Then she rolled her window down and tossed the rest out.

"Oops, messy boy." She grabbed my hand and nibbled on the tip of my pinky and then lapped it with her tongue. She did the same with my thumb. It actually tickled and I pulled it back. She laughed and then looked towards the infield as if listening for something. A car with a bad muffler broke the silence as it sped by on Bridge Road. Was it outrunning a cop who would give up because he saw us?

Angel leaned back and closed her eyes. I was boring her, all right. "So, where are you going to college?" I asked.

"Want to hear a secret?" Her eyes stayed closed. "I've been offered full rides at Tennessee, Georgia and Florida State, but I haven't picked one yet. I want to play out west in the Pac 12." Her words became whispers. "My dream school is UCLA, but they haven't sent a scout yet to watch me play."

How could I even respond to that? "Sounds like a good plan to get out of Pond Bridge. I can't wait to get out of here too." We had that in common. I would build on it.

"And one other thing." I could barely hear her. "Promise not to tell anyone?"

"I promise."

"The Georgia coach told me I'd be good enough to try out for the Olympic team by the time I was a junior there."

The future raced through my head. Would I manage all of her public appearances? Or maybe I could be a star runner, and we'd both make the Olympics. Our engagement photo would make the cover of Sports Illustrated. I looked up at the track and knew better. Only one of us had been given an Olympic body.

While her eyes were closed I used the chance to look at her as much as I wanted. The little bit of light from the parking lot gave heavy shadows and made all of her features stand out more, like a black and white photo. Her nose was soft. A tiny silver chain graced her neck. The collar on her shirt had shifted to the right, showing a little more skin near her collarbone. I could only see the upper part of her legs. Teardrop-shaped quadriceps fit just under the steering wheel. *Be a man*, it echoed in my head, but it was followed by *Violators will be prosecuted!*

Even though it was the most romantic—actually the *only* romantic moment—of my life, it was just another night out for her. I'd just enjoy the silence and not let anything mess it up. I lowered my breath so I could hear hers. It was slower than mine. Her heartbeat was too, because mine was probably shaking the truck.

"I'm thinking about getting my bellybutton pierced," she said.

I should have made my move when I had the chance.

"Did you see that picture of us from lunch the other day?"

"No." Of course I'd seen the picture. *They rubbed it in my face as soon as you posted it. Now I'm a meme. Why did you do that?*

She opened her eyes and tightened her posture before turning on the faded dome light. It was a miracle that thing worked. "Here, look."

Oh, I was. She lifted her shirt a few inches above her jeans. Purple fabric lined just under the denim of her waistline. My adrenaline shivering problem was about to kick in.

"I'd get a little loop right here." She pointed to the top of her navel.

"That might be dangerous while playing softball," I said. What was I, her dad?

"You know, I didn't think about that," she said and then lowered her shirt. "You should come to a game sometime."

She had an away game on Tuesday and Wednesday, and a home game on Thursday against Carissa's team, Perry South. I had kept the article from Dad's newspaper. Actually, I'd dug it out of the trash and dusted the coffee grinds off before preserving it under my bed. I knew half their schedule. I knew her class schedule. I'd found a copy of the team's practice schedule. "Well, do you have any home games this week?"

"One, I think." She got her phone out of her pocket. The lock screen had so many notifications she had to scroll through to see them all. Twitter, texts, missed calls—and at that moment, I was more important than any of them. Her fingers didn't seem to connect with the screen very well, but eventually she announced, "Wednesday the fourteenth, home against South Perry."

"I think the fourteenth is a Thursday."

"Yeah, that's what I said. The fourteenth against. . ." She tried to zoom in on the screen.

"South Perry. And Brian's girlfriend."

"Who's that?"

"Carissa Kelly," I said.

"Oh yeah, I love her!" Angel laughed and leaned her head towards my lap. There was a weird scent I'd never encountered. Some sort of smoky candle, or maybe some exotic incense I probably couldn't pronounce. Her ponytail batted my arm as she leaned back in her seat again.

Her phone was still out, so she saw the text message that came. "Oh shit, that's right. Want to come with me to a party?"

"Where at?" I could check it out, walk home if it was trouble. I'd never been to a real party before, but tonight was about firsts.

"Just on the other side of Pineville," she said and started typing her reply.

Pineville was past Perry and unless I was ready to run a marathon, there was no way of getting home on foot. "I'd better not," I said. I couldn't call Dad in the middle of the night. How would I visit Mom's grave every day if I was grounded?

Angel shifted her mouth to one side, but then laughed at the next text that came in. "Last one before spring break," she said. "You sure?"

"Yeah, I've gotta take care of a bunch of stuff still, and. . ." My reason didn't matter. She started the truck and drove it off the field before accelerating back into town. I had to remind her which street was mine, and then she missed the driveway.

When she stopped to let me out, she didn't pop the emergency brake. Instead, she answered another text.

"Thanks again for the lift," I said like she was a cabbie.

"See ya."

I tripped over my wiffle ball bat on my way to the door.

11

Sleep laughed at me that night. My imagination pictured Angel in every scenario at the party I'd vetoed attending. Anything from naked keg stands to sitting alone and thinking about me. Who knew?

According to Brian's texts that I had ignored, Angel wasn't sober. He said he was worried about me riding away with her, but I think he was more upset with their new third wheel, who'd spent the rest of the night filling Brian and Carissa in on her six nieces and nephews. Angel had acted goofy, but I hadn't smelled alcohol on her. We were still getting to know each other, so how could I say she was acting weird or different?

The next two mornings it took a lot of willpower not to run out onto Edge Road. Luckily I didn't, because I would need as much energy as possible for Monday's track practice. Coach Bates said we'd be done early, but he had "a little gaaaaame" for us to play first.

We all lined up at the fifty-yard line of the football field. The flagpole ropes rattled from the wind, which carried a heavy dose of fertilizer. In the distance, the softball team took the field for their practice. I stared past Coach Bates as he walked up and down our line explaining the rules.

I hadn't seen Angel at school, but there was no mistaking her on the softball diamond. She wore a bright pink jersey, probably from one of her past summer league teams. Whoever she was playing catch with was having a tough time with how hard she was throwing. Each time she caught one of Angel's fireballs, I could hear the synthetic leather of her glove snap.

Meanwhile, Katy meandered her way towards me in line. She sported a red, white, and blue windbreaker. Josh stood beside me and when he saw her, he put his hand over his heart and recited the Pledge of Allegiance. That seemed to keep her at a safe distance.

"The game is tag," Coach Bates said.

"I've heard of this one!" Katy said. "I have six nieces and nephews to play with, but the youngest two can't run yet."

"Then you'll be it for the girls," Coach said.

Everyone looked at me.

Max, our biggest teammate who held the school record in discus, jogged up late. Coach Bates pointed at him. "You'll be it as well."

This would be easy. Max was quick for a big guy, but tired easily. I expected Katy to chase me the whole time, but I had half a football field to elude her. She didn't have any stamina either. Despite her attempts to run distance with me, Coach had talked her into sprinting the shorter events.

We all spread out between the four cones on each side of the end zones and fifty-yard line. A pasture of freedom, until Coach Bates intervened. "And just to make it a little more interesting, my niece Skyler will be the third tagger." The team groaned. Skyler was a gazelle of a freshman who'd never lost a race in junior high. She pulled each wiry leg into her chest and hopped around.

"When you're tagged out, start running the hill. Last one in, no hills. Go!" Coach blew his whistle.

"Well this shouldn't take long," Josh said. "She's already got the scent of your pheromones locked in. Take a dive and let Max or Skyler tag you."

I looked back over to the softball practice. Angel was on the warmup mound just on the other side of the track fence. I watched her go into her windup and send the ball into the catcher's mitt. After a few pitches she looked my way.

Katy also noticed her. She saw my gaze and began digging her feet into the ground like a bull ready to charge.

After another shrill tweet of Coach Bates's whistle, we all scattered. Skyler loped towards a crowd and easily tagged three of them. Max caught a couple of the slower girls and was heading towards me. I jabbed left and shot right to the empty corner of the field. Katy was down on one knee like she was using a starting block, yet to go anywhere.

Somewhat alone, I caught my breath and watched Skyler dismantle pride from one boy at a time. Even Josh slipped and fell down. So many were tagged out that Coach realized he had made it too hard. The whistle blew again.

"Okay, that was pathetic," he said. "Everyone who's out already has five hills. Skyler, you're done too."

Half a football field to elude Katy and Max? I waved so long to Josh as he and the others began running the hill that the home bleachers sat on. Now was my chance to send a message to Katy: You'll never get me.

"Hold on," Coach Bates said, taking the whistle back out of his mouth. He jogged to one of the cones. "We gotta shrink this field down now that we have fewer people." He did the same on the other side.

"Uh-oh," someone mumbled. The wind picked up as a cloud covered a no-longer-beautiful afternoon. I glanced over at the hill, but most of my teammates had stopped at the top to rest and watch. To the other side, Angel still pitched on the practice mound in the bullpen area. She wasn't exactly facing us, but I knew I was visible. Meanwhile, much closer, Katy was clapping her hands together while high-stepping along the back border. I looked around at the other contenders. They seemed loose and worry-free, like it was just a simple game at track practice.

"Okay, on my whist— Katy, what are you doing?" Coach Bates dropped his whistle against his chest. Katy, eyes closed and once again in her own fantasy world, was now pretend kissing her right hand. She slinked her shoulders a few times and then finally licked her index finger. Coach Bates looked at Max. He had no answer, so he just shrugged and blew his whistle, and the showdown began.

Katy raced towards me, but I easily faked her out and jogged to where the cones bordered the thirty-yard line. Max cornered a few of the remaining players and surprised them with another burst of speed. Katy even funneled some runners back towards him, and I was one of the final people left. Only one other teammate stood between me and my predator, who was now snarling like some sort of wild animal from the African plains. Max took a charge at me, and I considered giving up to the consolation of second place, but over his right shoulder I spotted Angel pausing from her pitching to observe. Her gloved hand was on her hip. More adrenaline kicked in, and I felt like I still had all of my strength. Both of them keyed in on me. This gave the other final competitor, a quick little sophomore named Tim, a chance to catch his breath. The rest of the team abandoned the hill and was now cheering from just outside the boundary.

"Get 'im, Katy!" somebody yelled. A few other calls were made encouraging her even further.

"I must have you!" Katy yelled.

"Easy, girl," Max said. "Let me go in first." He approached slowly as I backed towards a corner.

"Stay in bounds, Lender," Coach said.

I tried my usual jab left, dash right tactic that had gotten me this far. I was just about past Max and had him stutter-stepping when he lunged with his left leg. My toe caught the tip of his ankle and I spun to the grass. My head bounced against the ground with such force that my ears rang.

When I was nine I almost choked to death on some pizza during Brian's birthday party. I went blue, gasped for air helplessly, and even lost my vision for a moment. His father eventually noticed and shoved his fists into my gut so hard that the pizza shot eight or nine feet across the room. I mention this because the impact of Katy leaping on me was ten times worse. She actually bounced off of me, her forehead smashing my left temple. My ribs cracked like they were knuckles, and the little wind I had was knocked out of me. I lay on my back, dazed and damaged. She hopped up and straddled me with one foot next to each of my hips, like a wrestler about to perform a finishing move.

"Get her off!" someone yelled, probably Josh. Katy tried to lower herself onto me. I curled into the fetal position, protecting my head like a building was about to collapse. When her shadow went away I finally released my face and sat up. Coach Bates had a hold of Katy's arm, practically dragging her away while she laughed and screamed, "I got him!" I turned my head towards the softball field, but Angel wasn't there.

Was all that for nothing?

"I guess Ted wins," Max said.

Still slightly dazed, I got to my knees. "She's gone?" I said, staring towards the softball field.

"She's over there with Coach," Josh said.

My senses were returning. "That was bullshit," I said. The rest of the team laughed, and a few gasped, as I climbed to my feet. A grass stain extended from my shoulder to my knee.

"Mark—" Coach started. It looked like he had placed Katy in timeout on a nearby bench.

"I know, I didn't win. I'll do my hills," I said.

"Actually if you could just not—"

"I said I'll do them!" I stumbled and then went into a jog towards the slope. Murmurs faded behind me as I pumped my arms up the steep incline. I watched the grass below me the whole way up and down. Fury makes excellent fuel sometimes. By the fourth time up the hill, I was breathing as hard as in a race. I stopped at the top with a better view. It was still cloudy and the temperature kept dropping. Rain was inevitable. I could smell it. I wished I could just sit down like the cows.

With my hands on my head I looked back down across the track towards the softball field. Angel was standing in the infield. The rest of the team formed a semicircle around her as she gestured in what must have been a pep-talk to them. A few deep breaths later the rage continued to evaporate from me. A huddle formed around Angel and the shout of "team" echoed before they all trotted towards the dugout ahead of her. What a view—over a hundred yards away, but I could watch her undisturbed. It wasn't as intimate as the belly shot, but seeing her made everything with Katy... worth it?

What would it take to get her lips on mine again? My torturous imagination insisted that she'd probably kissed someone at the party I hadn't gone to. She'd probably done more than that. While I lay nestled in my little boy bed, she'd probably seduced some college guy in a fancy bedroom of two parents who weren't home. "Never a chance," I mumbled.

I caught my breath as the rest of the track team trotted a cooldown. I scanned the softball field one last time. Angel turned, faced me and waved.

Maybe she'll change.

.

12

I pestered Coach Bates on Thursday to give us a short practice. "Got some studying to do, Mark?" he said, looking over my shoulder. The bleachers by the softball field were already filling up a half-hour before game time. The older generation of Pond Bridge carried blue and green blankets, thermoses of hot chocolate, and lawn chairs.

He wouldn't be happy until I admitted it. "Fine," I said. "I want to see the game against South Perry."

"Oh, suddenly a softball fan? Wonder why. Who's your favorite player?"

I didn't respond.

Eventually he sent us on a three-mile loop, but told us to slow our pace because of Saturday's invitational meet. I disobeyed his instructions and bat-out-of-helled it the whole time. In under twenty minutes, I was back on school grounds. I signaled Coach from afar, and he waved me off to the game.

I scanned the bleachers until I found Brian. His aged face blended well with the older crowd. I walked up the aisle and sat on the cold metal next to him.

"Beautiful day for a game," he said. The wind swept across our faces, and I shivered in my t-shirt. While running in the sun, I had been warm and a little sweaty. Now, in the shade, the dampness in my shirt worked against me.

"She's been nervous all week," Brian said as we watched Carissa finish her warm-up pitches on the mound. "Is Angel?"

"How the hell would I know?" He was mocking me. Game on. Suddenly Angel's voice erupted in a cheer from the dugout. "What time is it?"

"Game time!" the rest of the team screamed back. The two squads switched positions as Angel took the mound to start the game. I felt so miniscule and distant, like I was watching her on television. Her uniform was an immaculate white with blue trim that matched her visor. Her gold hair was in a tight French braid and black grease was smeared under each eye. The way she wound up and unleashed each pitch with such strength and accuracy fascinated me. Her throwing arm was a blur.

"You can barely see the ball. How are they going to hit that?" I asked. Each pitch gave a loud pop in the catcher's mitt.

"Oh don't worry, Carissa's not planning on giving up many hits either," Brian said.

"So I guess a double-date is probably out of the question after this one." I meant it as a joke.

"No, they're friends," Brian said. "The biggest obstacle would be getting you to ask Angel along."

Brian pointed to a guy in a bright orange Tennessee jacket. "See that? I think he's scouting Carissa." I could've confirmed it, because Angel had already been offered a full ride from there. It was my secret to keep, though.

"We almost had a moment the other night." I was starting to shiver from a combination of nerves and the cold.

"Almost? Did you kiss her?" The game began as Angel whipped fastballs into the strike zone.

"Shh!" I lowered my voice. "She's a pretty big deal here, if you can't tell." I thought I saw one of the old men two rows in front of us look back our way. "I think I could have, but I chickened out."

"What, would she have let you?" Just then the umpire grunted out a called strike three. I clapped along with the other fans. "Or what if she was into it. Then what?"

"I don't know. I guess I would've kissed her and then gotten out of the truck knowing what it's like." Thinking about it, I stopped shivering. The next batter fouled the first pitch off, but swung right through the next two.

Brian acted bored. "What if she would've kept going, though? Because usually. . ."

This was both my least and most favorite scenario. "I don't know. I mean, we were in my driveway in her truck, so. . ." I rocked back a bit nervously and bumped the knee of someone behind me.

"I know what I would've done in that situation. I got halfway there after we dropped you-know-who back off at the Gasmart." The third batter hit a soft fly ball to right field to end the top of the first. "By the way, if you ever go missing, I know whose basement to check."

"Thanks. Bring a pickaxe," I said. I escaped his questions as Carissa took the mound and his attention.

She was throwing almost as much heat as Angel, but with a softer, less intimidating look. No visor, no grease under the eyes, and she didn't tower over the others. Her pigtails stayed stiff after each toss. Still, her mechanics were smooth and effective.

Carissa disposed of the first two batters in under ten pitches, but all conversation halted as Angel got up to bat with two outs and nobody on. The first pitch was a fastball that caught the outside corner for a strike. Angel smirked at the ump, but then stepped back up to the plate. Her movements in the batter's box appeared so fluent and refined. My eyes outlined every inch of her tall frame. On the second pitch, Carissa fooled her with a changeup, causing Angel to swing way too soon and almost lose her balance. She gave her opponent a "you got me" smile, but then dug back in for the 0-2 pitch.

"The nice thing about these games is that when the pitching is this good, they don't take that long," Brian said. He rubbed his hands together for warmth. We both held our breaths as the next pitch was delivered. Angel turned on it with a textbook swing pulling the ball into deep left field before it slammed into the chain-link fence. She was rounding second as the outfielder threw a bullet towards third. She slid headfirst under the tag and pointed to the dugout as they cheered for her.

"Wow," I said. "That ball was drilled." I speculated how far she'd be able to hit one of the wiffle balls in my backyard. I caught myself clapping even louder with the crowd. I attempted a whistle, but my lips were too cold. Carissa shook her head and then struck out the next batter. Brian countered my applause.

"Traitor," I said.

"Angel got all the way to third base in no time," he said. I thought nothing of it at first. "One small adjustment and she would've made it all the way to home. A home run. . . All the way. . . Scoring."

His words bounced around in my head. "Yeah, yeah, smartass. I see what you're doing here."

"Seriously, Mark. What would you have done?"

"Not really worried about it," I said. "I'm not just some guy out to get some, and for all the effort you're putting into it. . ."

"Something wrong with that? I'm a seventeen-year-old man, aren't I?" His tone changed. "No offense, but we can't spend every Saturday night playing video games for the rest of our lives," he said. "You're seriously scared to make love to a woman, aren't you?"

"That's like asking me if I'm afraid to fly to the moon. It's not going to happen, so why do I have to worry about it?" Now I was using similes too.

"Scared, worried, same thing."

I crossed my arms and leaned forward. "Yes, then. I'm scared. Terrified. I don't know what the hell I'm doing. I don't want to get anyone pregnant. Plus. . ." There had to be a plus. "I'm not in love with her." The word seemed ricochet off his face. "Oh, is Brian in looove?"

"Of course I'm in love," he said. "I love her very much."

The argument ended with both of us feeling victorious, or at least satisfied. Brian even bought me a hot chocolate when he noticed my lips were turning blue. The strikeouts were piling up for both sides, so there wasn't a lot of action. Brian leaned back to the row of bleachers behind us, and we barely spoke for a few innings. The pitcher's duel continued as our moods lightened back up. A few singles for each team yielded a 1-1 tie into the seventh.

"I hope it doesn't go into extra innings," Brian said. At this point I was freezing, starving, and nervous for Angel all at the same time. She had been walked in her last two at-bats because Carissa refused to throw her anything she could hit. If Angel could pitch three more outs, she'd get one more chance to hit in the last inning.

With two outs and a runner on third, Carissa stepped up to the plate. Brian crossed his fingers and jerked his head with each pitch. Angel blew a fastball by her to make it a 2-2 count. There was no way she was going to catch up to the fastball.

"One more like that," I mumbled.

"We'll see," Brian said. It was the same language we used during our hours of video games. Neither of us ever openly taunted the other, but the silent wars of who beat who on whatever day got psychologically vicious. Today the competition was out of our control.

"Choke up on the bat!" the South Perry coach yelled from her spot behind third base. "Scoot back in the box."

"She should throw a changeup," I whispered to Brian. "She'll be so far in front of it. . ."

Angel must've been thinking the same thing. She exaggerated her wind-up as her arm seemed to move in the same blur as it always did, but upon release, the ball fluttered in softer. Carissa double-clutched and waited to make perfect contact. Any other hitter would have struck out, but Carissa's bat slammed the ball, and it sailed into the left-center field gap. The leading run scored.

Angel bit the top of her glove after the play was over. It was odd but intriguing to see her so upset at herself. I watched a half-dozen expressions on her face that I'd never witnessed before. Regret, doubt, and anger all debuted in her eyes. But just as quickly as they arrived, with one swipe of her glove across her face, the rage was quelled. While she struck out the next batter, I daydreamed what it would be like to be happy together. Or sad together. Or both upset with the outcome of our favorite television show on a Friday night where we'd decided to order delivery pizza and wear fuzzy sweatpants together. We would be the same height while lying down, but then she'd want to take things further, and— Brian was one-hundred percent right. I was terrified.

Carissa walked the first batter of the inning, which roused the home dugout. The fans thawed a bit too, but it was hard for them to clap with gloves on. "This is pretty damn exciting, isn't it?" Brian said. "No matter who wins, I really enjoyed watching."

"Me too," I said. Was he kidding? I wanted Angel to win this game more than anything. He was only saying that as insurance. Had Carissa dominated the game, he'd be throwing snide comments at me, and the afternoon would've been ruined.

An out later, Angel was up to bat. On the second pitch, an inside fastball, she shifted her hips into a swing and pulled the ball down the left field line. It flew much higher than her triple in the first inning. The dugout screamed. She galloped towards first, watching the ball sail towards the fence. At the last second, it hooked foul, clearing the fence by ten feet. Halfway down the baseline, she squatted, stood back up, and calmly returned to the plate. She wiggled the bat in her hands like it was as light as the plastic bat in my yard.

Brian looked at me and we both exhaled a laugh. This was better than any video game we'd ever gone head-to-head in. With the count at one ball and one strike, the cheers from the dugout got even louder. Brian clenched his fists and leaned forward. Carissa looked to the catcher's signals for the next pitch, but kept shaking it off. I found my entire body tensed up, and even though I didn't have the nerve to vocalize it, I was shouting for "my girl" in my head.

In the corner of my eye, Katy appeared at the bottom of the bleachers. "There you are," she said, "Right where we agreed to meet." She walked up the bleachers two rows at a time, causing a loud clomp. She sat right in front of us. "Who's winning?" she asked.

I looked at Brian to remind him this was his fault for picking her up the other day. He accepted the blame with a shrug. "2-1 Perry South," he said, maintaining his stare as the catcher jogged out to the mound to confer with Carissa.

"That's not a lot of points though, is it, Marky?"

What do you even say to that? "Nope. Close game, though," I said. Carissa prepared for the next pitch while Katy persisted with questions. I hated to acknowledge her, because she took it to heart like a wedding proposal.

"Do you like close games?" she asked.

Brian looked at me now like it was my fault. What was I supposed to do?

"Sure," I said. Ball two. A changeup that bounced before it hit the plate.

"What else do you like? Other close things?"

"Focusing on the game." Ball three, outside.

"Ohh, is that so?" Katy continued talking to herself—or me—but I kept my gaze on Angel as she tapped her bat on the heel of both of her cleats. Clumps of dirt dropped off. She looked over to get the signal from her third base coach, who was touching her hat and nose. I wondered what that meant and found even more admiration. To think, this girl was an expert at a game I knew very little about. My mediocre baseball career ended before high school. Even with a hundred at-bats, I'd be lucky to hit one ball into fair territory off of her.

The next pitch, ball four, almost grazed Angel on the knee. After her previous walks, Angel had always hustled over to first base. This time she set her bat down across the plate and walked like it was a Sunday afternoon in the park. It was the hottest thing I'd ever seen.

Now Carissa was showing a prism of emotions. She mouthed some words, obviously obscenities, into her glove, and threw the first pitch to the next batter over the catcher's head. Both Angel and the runner ahead of her advanced a base.

"I wish she'd calm down," Brian said. I stayed quiet as part of our unspoken truce.

"Sorry, Brian, but I'm not going to calm down," Katy said. "And if you have a problem with it, I'll shove this size thirteen boot up your ass!" Strike one to the next batter as Brian laughed.

Katy stood up and sat next to me. "Are you cold, Marky?"

Brian sighed. "Katy, can you please give us some guy time here? We were having a personal conversation."

Katy nodded and walked back down the bleachers.

"How did you do that?" I asked.

"Speak like an adult." I wasn't sure why he was terse with me. Time was called as the manager and the rest of the infielders all circled around Carissa to discuss strategy. South Perry brought their outfielders almost all the way in to just behind Angel at second base. Brian mumbled about it being a smart move, but I was still baffled.

All I had to do was tell Katy to go away and she would? Hadn't I made it clear? Maybe it was that Brian told her and not me. Who knows what they talked about after I bailed from ice cream the other night?

Angel's teammate stepped into the box as she cheered from second base. Carissa shook her head like there were kinks in her neck. Finally, she wound up and delivered.

Ding! A line drive shot off the bat into short right field and Angel was already rounding third. The first runner scored with no problem. The outfielder picked up the ball and heaved it all in one practiced motion. The catcher waited on the ball as both Angel and the white sphere flew towards home. She dove head first, spitting up a cloud of dust in the chilled air.

91

"Safe!" the umpire signaled, and Angel jumped up as her teammates stormed the field.

I was already standing and yelled with the rest of the crowd. Brian hit his fist into his hand and then shook mine, as if we had just played. "Good game," he said.

"Yes, good game, and if you want to look on the bright side, our school won, right?"

"I suppose so."

We emptied out of the bleachers with everyone else. I overheard people talking about what a brilliant game Angel had pitched, and how fast she had been on the winning run, and how great that slide was under the tag of the catcher, and how she would be playing on ESPN next year at this time. All of it was true.

Brian's keys jingled in his hand. "I'm actually going over to Carissa's for dinner," he said.

"Oh, I'll just text my dad for a ride." My numb fingers had trouble, but I eventually sent him the message.

"No use getting there before her," he said. We sat back down on the front row of bleachers as the last few people packed up their blankets.

"Let's say one or both of us has a serious relationship with these girls," I said.

"Let's say? I already do." His tone echoed the loss.

"Well, are you going to keep dating her once she's off at college next year? And then attend that college just because she's there?" I rubbed the goosebumps on my arms. "I mean, what if it's some expensive out-of-state school?"

"You aren't at that point yet," was his answer. "Talk to me when you get over your fear of girls." He was looking at Carissa now. Her team was a sad caravan hauling equipment back to the bus. He had some consoling to do.

I felt bad for a moment, but had he answered my legitimate question with an insult? I shrugged it off and went back into the school to get my books.

By the time I got back outside, the sun was setting. The South Perry bus was pulling out of the lot, and only a few cars remained. I walked over toward the school's pickup spot and leaned against the brick wall under the light. The blue pickup wasn't far away. Right then, Angel appeared, still in uniform. She carried her bat bag in one hand and her cleats in the other. Her dirt-stained socks were pulled down to her ankles just above her flip-flops. They smacked the pavement with each stride.

"Great game," I said. She smiled and walked over toward me. I felt my shoulder blades against the wall.

"Aww, thanks for staying through the whole thing."

"And for the record, I would've thrown her a changeup there too."

I don't know if it was the fact that I knew enough about pitching to make that statement, or if it was that I was one of the few students who'd cared enough to sit in the cold. Or maybe just the spring air and the sunset. Or maybe even the previous encounters we'd had. Right then, Angel dropped her bag and her cleats onto the pavement and put both of her hands behind my head and kissed me to heaven. Her tongue pressed against mine before I could even think about whether I was doing it right. I peeked and saw that her eyes were shut. I did the same. I listened to the little noises she made that would cycle from my ears to my heart for the rest of my life. Finally, she pulled back and smiled. I was so dazed that if she'd have punched me in the face, I would have worn the same stunned expression. She laughed a bit and looked at the ground.

A small honk came from a car nearby. "Nice timing, Dad," I said. We both laughed this time. She touched me on the nose and waltzed her stuff back to her truck. I watched her get in and drive off under the glare of the yellow lights. Behind where her truck was parked stood Katy. Her arms were crossed and her nostrils flared.

I hurried into Dad's car. "Looks like things are going well with your new friend," Dad said as I slung my backpack into the back seat.

I covered my face like I had been caught in the act of cheating on a final exam. "How could you tell?"

"Well, there's no lipstick this time, but you've got a chest full of infield dirt and grease under your eyes. You either played in the game or made out with the young lady who just left in that truck. Either way, looks like you got to first base."

I wiped my finger on my cheek. My fingertip was black.

"What would your mother have said?" He laughed a bit and then noticed my body language. "Bet she'd be proud."

I wasn't sure about that, but I'd ask in the morning.

13

Long before the birds sang their morning obligations, something other than my alarm woke me up. *She kissed me!* I lived it over and over until I realized there was no possibility or even desire to go back to sleep. The first one had been nothing. A simple peck to apologize. But the newest kiss was unmistakable, and the feeling of being liked—by someone other than Katy—got me out of bed with no problem. I felt my way into my running clothes and snuck out the front door.

The morning air was brisk but still. Neither pig nor cow manure dominated the town as I jogged up Main. I looked towards the sign at the bank. Fifty-three degrees at. . . 3:37? Oops. Was it really that early? I laughed a bit and increased my pace.

On the travel agency's cleavage poster, the two beautiful girls continued to keep their arms around the college guy and his abs. I continued north as I decided I didn't need them anymore. I would run on Edge Road again, but just a little. No one would know, and Coach Bates probably would only use me for the 800 at tomorrow's meet. I could recover enough to run two laps. I'd just run a mile on Edge Road, not all the way to her house.

I thought about Angel again and sped up. She had played so well, and there would be more pictures of her in the newspaper. I would buy my own copy and cut them out so that Dad wouldn't know.

The half-moon lit the way as I heard a cow moo from the field. It was too dark to see whether they were standing or not, but I'd turn around soon anyway. Without even the slightest chance at traffic, I ran down the middle of the road. It was just my feet against the pavement and the crickets, along with the occasional mooing. Being up at this hour felt like trespassing, but even if a cop showed up, I could explain that I was a track star. I thought back to how nervous I'd been when Angel and I were out on the softball field in her truck. After this season they could name the field after her.

On I went until I saw a light ahead on the right side of the road. I had run over a mile. Maybe two. Or was it more? The light got closer and I sped up even more. It was her house! Protected by the darkness, I slowed to a walk so that my feet stopped slapping the pavement. Set back off the road a bit, the home was large and square—a giant box on a country road with a huge porch that held the light. A detached garage next to the home housed all the vehicles, and the driveway had a basketball hoop with a glass backboard. Someday I would shoot hoops with her right there.

As I passed the house, I noticed the white circular sign cut out from the pine. All of the softball players had one. Home of Angel #20, it said.

I began to run again. Turning around here would've meant that her house was the only reason I ran this far. I increased my pace until I couldn't see the light from her porch anymore. "Who are you trying to fool?" I said into the darkness. I was probably halfway to Elk Falls.

I turned around and jogged back towards town. This was dumb. I had a meet in just over 24 hours. What was I going to gain by passing her house at four in the morning?

The Hayden residence appeared again. First the light, and then the square outline of the house. Everything still appeared dark gray from the shadows or yellow from the light. I should have turned around ten minutes ago when I got here. I'd be that much closer to town instead of miles away from home.

The house remained dark and silent. I was about to focus just on the road ahead of me when I did a double take. The blue pickup was now parked under the basketball hoop. My stomach dropped. Was she watching me? I sprinted the next little stretch of road and stopped. Maybe I had just overlooked it. Why would she be out so late on a school night? It was dark, so I probably just hadn't noticed the truck the first time. I had just been there.

My legs were the first part of me to demand answers. I let them lead me back towards the outskirts of the yard. *Go home*, I told myself, but I had to know. She'd kissed me, so it was my right to find this out. I crossed the front of the driveway and stood by the mailbox. It was a cold, metallic and oversized container. How many college recruiting letters filled it every day?

I looked at each window. My eyes had adjusted to the night long ago, and there seemed to be curtains or blinds at every opening. There certainly wasn't anyone looking out at me. I hunched over and scampered to the truck. It would give me the truth. Before my hand even touched it I could feel the warmth from the hood. My heart joined my stomach somewhere below my kidneys. I started to trot back towards the road in a direct line through the yard.

A light turned on behind me.

The fastest recorded 40-yard dash by any Pond Bridge native is 4.6 seconds. The record was established by a football player from twenty-some years ago after he played college football and was trying to get drafted in the NFL. He played a season and a half for Chicago, but then injured himself beyond repair. His speed is still talked about like folklore. That morning, I guarantee I smashed his record.

I didn't hear anything, so once it felt safe, I stopped and looked back. Actually, I almost puked, *then* stopped and looked back. The light was from the detached garage, and after another minute or so, it turned back off. Automatic motion-sensing light. I'd escaped undetected!

Running close to four more miles after that adrenaline flush felt like I was wearing a dozen wet blankets. Cold ones, too. The shivers grabbed me once again, but I was still riding my sense of relief. I laughed as I passed the cows. Back in town, I waved at the girls on the poster, and finally I crawled back into my driveway as the sky began to turn a hint of gray and a few raindrops sprinkled my face. My body slowly recovered, but the pit in my gut asked again, "Where had she been?" The question repeated over and over as I got ready for school.

That morning as I stepped onto the bus, I realized I had forgotten to visit the cemetery again.

***

The cows must have been sitting down that morning, because the rain continued throughout the day. It poured as the clock neared three, and during his afternoon announcements Mr. Mallett gave us runners some good news. "Track practice will be a brief meeting held in the cafeteria. Attendance is mandatory."

Not everyone heard the announcement, so a few of them still went and changed in the field house after school. It was down to a small drizzle at first, but then right as Coach Bates began to speak, the clouds opened and another downpour was underway. "Everybody here?" Coach asked. He had to repeat himself over the rain.

I knew one person who was missing. Maybe she quit or just skipped.

My hopes didn't get a chance to expand. Her shoes squeaked before she yelled, "I am so freaking soaking wet!" She reminded me of a stray cat my mother once bathed in a sink to help it get rid of its fleas—the cat wouldn't go away either.

"Should've listened to the announcement," Coach said. "Now, we'll get everyone out of here shortly. Here's who's running. It's an invitational, so we only get to enter two people per—"

98

His eyes grew as he looked in Katy's direction. "No!" One of the senior girls grabbed Katy right as she was pulling her pullover jacket off. Everything else had seemed to be coming with it.

Josh bumped my elbow. "You see that happy trail? Right click. Delete. Empty recycle bin. Are you sure? Yes."

I thought about Angel's abs instead and wondered if that picture was still online. After the commotion, Coach Bates finally announced who was running which events. Katy was not varsity, so she wouldn't run in this meet. For some reason, Coach felt it necessary to stress that everyone was welcome to ride the bus tomorrow morning to support those of us who were in a race. "Wait, I'm not done," he said. "Has anyone seen Ted?" Someone called out that Ted was sick. Coach Bates looked at his clipboard and scribbled something. "Tell ya what. Let's move Mark to the 3200, and Josh, you'll run the 800 now."

Two miles? How much regret could I fit into a morning workout? Josh was happy because that promoted him into the meet, but it pushed me to my least favorite event.

"Bus for Akron leaves at 7:30. Any questions?" Josh and I were two steps towards the door when Katy's hand shot up.

"Yes, Katy," Coach said. Everyone froze.

"Should people who are running the 3200, like Marky, drink a lot of milk tonight?"

The girl to Josh's left started muttering under her breath while everyone else laughed. "Honestly, what the hell is she talking about half the time?" I heard Bates's niece say.

"I bet she's got some milk for ya," one of the guys said. Bates told Katy no and ignored the crude answers.

"Hide me," I said to Josh. I jogged back into the hallway towards the gym, hopefully unnoticed. I peeked around the corner where Josh was actually talking to her. He pointed in the other direction, and Katy stomped towards the door where everyone else was exiting. The rain had let up some, so everyone rushed out to their cars. I texted Josh to wait up so I could get a ride back into town once it was safe. He said it wasn't yet.

To kill some time I went farther down the hall towards the windows that faced the softball field. Puddles coated the dirt. The entire team was huddled in one dugout. One by one they began running towards the building. I turned away as they passed me and scurried into the locker room, but there was no sign of Angel. Alone again, I looked back out to where the rain was now falling in sheets.

Like a goddess emerging from a waterfall, Angel appeared from the dugout. She was in no hurry, and even paused to look up into the sky while the drops rebounded off of her forehead. Her blue practice jersey clung to her tanned arms. Again she stopped and pushed the water out of her hair, perfectly accepting the drenching. I could've watched this movie for hours, but I realized she would be walking by me very soon. What would I say? I stutter-stepped and then galloped a stride back towards the cafeteria. I had to cement my feet to the floor and talk to her.

"Oh, hey," I said as she came inside. She was occupied with squeezing the water out of her hair. I waited until she was closer and then tried to get her attention.

"This is bullshit," she said.

That wasn't at me, was it? "Still practicing?"

"We still have to condition in the gym, apparently. Our coach thinks we're all fat-asses or something."

I laughed a little, but her scowl remained. There had to be a joke I could've made that complimented her ass, but it never developed. I was more distracted by the way her wet shirt stuck to her.

"Oh. Well, I've got my meet tomorrow." Drops of water raced down her cheeks. What if I could tell her something so wonderful that tears would do the same? "It's in Akron, if you—"

"Hayden, get changed!" her coach yelled from down the hall.

"I gotta go," she said. She brushed against my arm, leaving it wet. I raised it and wiped the moisture onto my cheek. Her rubber cleats chirped down the hallway. I was alone again.

But I wasn't.

"Hole. E. Shit!" Josh yelled from across the empty cafeteria. "Are you banging her?"

I ran at him before he could yell anything else. "No, of course not."

"But you want to."

"What? No. Why would you think that?"

"I know what I just saw."

The cheeks I'd dampened with Angel's rain water were now on fire. "Can I get a ride?"

"Tell me the truth first."

"Fine."

On the way home I explained to Josh what had been going on and what had happened after the game.

"You're going straight to the major leagues, slugger," he said. "You could be set for prom." The more his voice escalated, the more I tried to downplay everything.

"We're just hanging out some."

"No one just hangs out with her, Mark. She's not the kinda girl who just likes to make out and roll around with her shirt off."

"She's not?" That sounded like the best idea ever.

"No, man. She's down with, like, college guys."

"So guys that are seven or eight years older than your girl?"

"Don't change the subject." He plugged his phone into the dashboard. "I would've never guessed you and Angel, though."

"Why not?"

"Leah maybe, but Angel?"

"At least she'll keep Katy away. I'm so sick of her stalking me all the time. She'll probably be hiding in the bushes later tonight."

"Stop trying to change the subject." We sped into town in Josh's dealership SUV of the month. "You're gonna get laa-aaid," he sang.

"No, I'm not. Stop it." I shifted in the huge passenger seat. Warm air from the vents blasted against me.

"What are you afraid of? Trust me, she'll guide you right through it, I bet. And once she finds out you're a virgin. . ."

I guessed that was public knowledge with a guy like me.

"Once she knows that, man, you are *set!*" We pulled into my street. "You won't even have to try. Dammit, I'm jealous. I gotta buy bracelets and shit for my girl, and it probably still won't work."

"She doesn't just sleep with anyone, Josh. No girl does." We were almost to my house. "That's not what I'm after anyway."

"That's true, she has said no before."

I didn't need confirmation on this. We pulled into my driveway as I became offended on her behalf.

"She's shot Jefferson down a dozen times," he said.

"She has?"

I love her.

14

There was a chance Angel was in the crowd. I could not lose my race.

The bleachers were scattered with colors from the ten different districts that competed in the Akron Invitational. Most of them were high schools not much larger than Pond Bridge, so I wasn't going up against North-Central Ohio's all-time greatest.

The morning was cool and dry with the sun only showing itself on occasion. My feet felt like springs as I loosened up on the spongy track. My warmup pants swished in time.

"First call, men's 3200-meter run," announced the PA. I spotted Dad along the short fence at the top of the first turn. He had a coffee in one hand and a rolled up newspaper in the other. He wore his only Pond Bridge High sweatshirt for the occasion.

Next to Dad was Josh's father, Bill. His made-for-TV face stuck out among the others. He was dressed in Eddie Bauer clothing with no hint of school spirit. Team Khaki for Mr. Harding. I was impressed that Dad and a few of the other parents were cool enough to stand by him. I guess hanging out with the "common folk" helped Bill's image, which led to more vehicle sales.

I paused my warm-up for some words of advice. "Plenty of wind on that backstretch," Dad said.

"Yep." I nodded and scanned the area for Angel. The concession stand wasn't too far away, and the scent of popcorn wafted towards us.

Mr. Harding greeted me with a firm handshake like we'd just completed a deal on a used Ford. "Josh running the 800 today?"

"I wanted to trade, but he wasn't having it." Now I felt cool too.

"Is your friend here?" Dad asked. He sipped his coffee trying to hide his smile.

"My friend?"

"Bill, I go to pick this kid up the other day and you know that softball stud, Angel Hayden's her name? Well, she's got him against the wall. . ."

I jogged off as the PA announced second call. I went around the high jump pit and across the grass towards the starting line. My veins flowed with adrenaline. I piled my warmup pants and shirt near the other racers' stuff. The cold air chilled my arms and legs. I untucked my solid green tank top jersey from my blue shorts and re-laced my shoes. I felt skinny. I *was* skinny.

"Final call, men's 3200-meter run." Nine other antelope-framed boys lined up with me on the arc-shaped starting line. Patches of acne and thin facial hair seemed to be in style. After a brief intro and the shot from the starter gun, we were off.

While running through the first turn, I always made sure not to get tripped. With a two-mile race, there's no hurry to get to the front. I tucked myself behind a few of the leaders, and we contended with the brutal wind on the backstretch.

I looked right to see Katy pressed against the small fence, her head leaning over as she screamed, "Go Marky! Run for me!" Was it my imagination or did another runner actually chuckle at this?

At the next turn I started to eye the bulk of the crowd in the first few rows of bleachers. There was someone in a jacket with her hood up who might have been Angel. Her gloved hands clapped, and she was wearing green, but I wasn't sure. She cradled a blue blanket in her right arm.

104

"Seventy-two, seventy-three," the pacer read off as we completed lap one. We were all too fast, but I felt good. I felt great even. The field slowed down. I didn't.

"Pace yourself!" Dad yelled right as I took the lead. If Angel traveled all this way to see me. . .

The wind on the backstretch blew harder and seemed to pass right through my ribs. I slowed down to save a little energy.

"Yeah, Marky! Give it to me!" Katy yelled. Did I have a whole season of this to put up with? "Boo! You're going to lose!" she called out to the guys right behind me.

Welcome to my hell, everyone else.

I rounded the turn still in the lead and zeroed in on the girl I thought was Angel. From fifty yards out I was sure it was her. An extra dose of adrenaline released into my bloodstream. The closer I got, the more sure I was. A moment later she turned and seemed to morph into someone else. It was a mother holding a baby in a blanket!

I really needed to see an eye doctor. And reality. I was surprised my own father went to the trouble of showing up for this one, so why would she? Fatigue and doubt started to creep in, but I battled through each lap. That's all distance running really was—a boxing match between me and that voice in my head telling me it's okay to slow down.

The lead pack caught up with me as we completed the first mile in 5:27. My breathing and heart rate were much higher than during my morning runs. My leg muscles began to feel like they were drowning, but I fought through to stay near the lead. A side cramp developed, but those were common at this pace.

Katy's encouragement grew crazier.

Lap five: "Win this and I'll marry you!" Definitely anti-motivational.

Lap six: "Do it for me, and I'll do it for you!" Maybe I could get a pole vaulter to hit her.

Lap seven: "Show them why you're the king of my world!" You're the queen of insanity.

Lap eight: "Win this and I'll give you my jersey right here!" No one in the lead pack wanted that and with two hundred meters to go, the front three pulled away. I tried to start my kick, but the signal to go faster didn't reach my legs. I felt every unnecessary stride that I'd taken yesterday at four in the morning.

I crossed the finish line and collapsed in the grass, exhausted and embarrassed. I could hear the other runners who beat me laughing about my obnoxious fan. I sat up.

"Good race, Mark." Coach Bates extended his hand. "11:18, which I believe is a PR for you."

I looked up and nodded that it was. My breathing finally slowed, and I hurried to put my warm-ups back on before the post-adrenaline chills set in. Coach Bates still had his hand extended. I grabbed it to get up. He congratulated me on fourth place and trotted off to time the women's 3200.

The shivering began as I walked back towards Dad and Bill Harding.

"Guess those morning runs are paying off," Dad said. I nodded as my teeth chattered.

"Here you go," Bill said, handing me a hot chocolate.

"Thanks," I said. My breathing was finally back to normal and the foam cup felt warm against my hand. I took a big swig.

"Some girl bought that for you," he said.

Dad laughed. "The boy's got a lot of female fans, what can I say?"

Katy's cheering echoed in my head. "Thanks for coming out. I'm going to go die on the bus real quick," I told them both and then walked away. I exited the track area and tossed almost the full hot chocolate into the trash. I'd thought it tasted funny.

As I was getting back onto the bus, Josh was getting off. "I'm an idiot," I said.

"Get lost during your race? How many times have I told you? It's turn left," he said, running in a small circle.

"A few private schools beat me."

"Yeah, that happens. That's why my parents insist on sending me to public."

I smiled but went on to explain my error in pacing. I failed to tell him why, but I knew the truth. What kind of a moron runs eight miles the day before a race? I vowed never to run out on Edge Road again. And for me to even think that Angel would be at the race had been ridiculous. She was probably puking out a hangover. And with the hot chocolate from Katy that I had sipped, I'd probably be puking soon too.

***

I warmed up on the bus and returned to the fence to watch Josh's race with Dad. Schmoozing with Bill Harding couldn't hurt either. I felt safe between them.

Katy was the only one on the team not in a race but still in attendance. She even did warm-up sprints on the backstretch when it was open. I eluded her until the bus ride home.

We were speeding down I-71, a smelly bus full of gassed athletes. I sulked some more because I know I could've won that race. Maybe the newspaper would've done a story on me. Angel would have noticed. Maybe her dad would be excited about her dating me. Maybe colleges would start sending *me* recruiting letters. I had to train smarter. No more running on Edge Road. It's like Mom knew I would be in this situation ten years ago when she made that declaration. There would be plenty of other races, but now Coach Bates would stick me in the 3200 every meet. I was rewinding the last few laps in my head trying to change the outcome when Katy walked towards the back of the bus. Josh nudged me, but I was already on guard.

"Everyone's attention, please." She raised her hand for a public declaration. "You should congratulate Marky on his fourth-place prize."

No. They shouldn't. And they didn't. Impressive. Not one teammate even giggled. Katy looked around. Her jersey was stretched to the stitches over her sweatshirt, and she began pulling it off.

"Is that my sweatshirt?" I said.

"Marky, do you need a water? Or how 'bout a banana?"

"You don't have either of those, and no. I want my sweatshirt back."

Katy smiled and nodded. "You gave it to me." A few teammates laughed, and the bus become a hundred degrees warmer. Where had I left it? She didn't take it from my locker, and as far as I knew, she hadn't broken into my house. Yet.

"I never gave it to you. Where'd you get it?" It was the most direct I'd been to her. I looked her straight in the glasses above her crooked smile.

"Maybe it was the night we went out for ice cream together. I don't know, we've done so much."

"Wait, what?" Josh said.

Others surrounded her like she was a celebrity sharing stories at a house party. She glanced to each side, totaling her audience and opportunity. "I mean, it was on my bedroom floor after you left."

"You're full of shit!" I yelled.

"Language," Coach Bates called out. Why hadn't he kept her up front?

Others looked on. I even saw a girl recording the whole thing on her phone. The sun shone through my window, and the bus was boiling.

"I've never been to your house. I left it downtown," I said, pointing. I recalled the morning that I dropped it on the bench on Main and forgot to pick it up at the end of my run.

"For me," she said. "You left it for me. Be honest." She folded her arms to work as a lock, but I wasn't about to fight it off of her. Then she lifted the front and inhaled. With her eyes closed, she absorbed every ounce of sweat saturating that thing. "Smells like my Marky."

"You even want it back?" Skyler asked. A fair question, but yes. After purification, of course.

"Didn't he cheat on you?" Josh asked.

I glared at him, but he nodded with a look of insight.

"He did," Katy said. Everyone was still captured by her. "Right in front of me, he kissed Angel Hayden, and I'll hate her forever."

They all asked each other if it was true, and then went straight to their phones like the answer was on Snopes. I stayed neutral in my expression. My teammates started to laugh and mumble again about how crazy Katy was. Josh whispered to me that he had it under control. "Oh, so you don't question Nutjob here when she says Mark was in her room, but you don't think he'd kiss Angel?"

"Well. . ." I said, but I didn't have the words to finish the sentence.

Josh continued. "I saw it too. Katy's just jealous." He sat back down, and I almost hugged him. She stormed back to the front of the bus, but my teammates were still looking at me.

"I have other sweatshirts," I said.

15

When I awoke, it was still black outside. I didn't want to know what time it was. My window was open and the crickets taunted me. The last lap of the race still lingered in my head. I had to train smarter, yet a half-hour later I was jogging past the cows less than a mile from Angel's house.

No meets were scheduled for the week because of spring break, so I had plenty of time to recover. Practices were optional, but I could get so many more useful miles sticking to my routine. The road just happened to be a mostly flat, low-trafficked area, so why not take advantage? There were no plans to enter her yard again. From here on out, her house was just another building that I passed on my way.

A scary thought hit me as I saw the front porch light in the distance. Had I been a few minutes later on Friday morning, she would've passed me on the road. No sooner did the thought of this potential catastrophe strike me, than I heard a rumbling from behind. An engine was approaching and headlight beams peeked over the small slope of the road.

I squinted in the thin moonlight to see the ditch to my left. I took a giant step over it, but my foot slid in the mud. I waved my arms like a tightrope walker and leaned away from the road. It was still too close, so I lunged another step and *zap!* An electric fence sent enough volts through me to paralyze my body for a brief moment. I shook it off, then ducked into the weeds, my right foot completely submerged into a sludgy mess. Was the vehicle slowing down? Mosquitos set up an all-you-can-eat buffet on my limbs and neck, but I couldn't risk movement for a few more seconds. A gnat sang in my ear. Then I could even hear the vehicle's stereo pumping a quick bass. The car, an old beat-up hatchback, passed by me and the Hayden residence. I should've known it wasn't her. Both headlights worked.

I lunged back up to the road. My legs itched, my feet were muddy, but I kept running. I raced past the house without the intention of traveling much farther. Her truck slept in the driveway, and the home was dormant. If I reversed direction now, I could get back before Dad woke up. Before I could make my U-turn back towards town, I heard a door slam. Or was it something else? I kept running in case anyone saw me. For another half-mile I kept looking right and left for a safer ditch if I needed it. I was over five miles from home by the time I stopped panicking.

I couldn't keep going. My shoes were a mess, my feet were soaked, and I was tired. Someday I'd tell our grandkids about all this. Meanwhile the lactic acid from yesterday's race was setting in. My calves screamed for a break. Why hadn't I bothered to run a cooldown?

I started back towards the house and my panic resumed. It was starting to get light out. The longer I waited, the riskier it would be. I even contemplated spending the whole day out in the country until it was safe to pass at nightfall. It was either dash now or spend a day with nature. A missing person report wasn't the best way to gain attention.

I gathered my wits and picked up the pace as best I could. The house looked different with just a little more light. It was a soft blue, and white trim bordered the sides. The closer I got, the faster I ran. I focused on an imaginary finish line a quarter mile down and raced towards it. The sun was my competitor today. If I didn't look at her house, maybe no one would look out at me. My breathing didn't contribute to anything stealthy. The cramping began. I expected one of the Haydens to yell something at me—please don't let it be Angel or Leah! I blew by the mailbox and took once glance left.

The truck was missing. What kind of weird hours did this girl keep? I knew it had just been there. And now it was gone. I looked up to the sky for answers, but it only grew bluer.

By the time I reached town, my pace was a walk. The sun was up, cars were driving to church, and I had mud up to my ankles. When I got to the gates of the cemetery, something told me to turn around and just go home. Mom didn't want to see me like this.

***

'Staycation' is a bullshit word. Brian vacationed with Carissa's family. The Hardings spent the bulk of their week in the Caribbean. Even Willie's family went up to Lake Erie for a few days. I was stuck at home because Dad's school wasn't off until the following week. All I had were my memories of Angel.

I grew more careful on my runs. For example, on Tuesday I ran at night, and didn't even go all the way up to her house. I approached only close enough to see that her truck was still missing, but a few lights were on in the house. Once I even saw a nicer truck parked in the garage, which someone had left open. After that, I turned around. I flirted with disaster as well as I flirted with girls.

By Friday morning I'd convinced myself that she was over me. There was no way to contact her. Was she on more college visits? Or maybe a vacation too? But what kind of vacation would she go on without her parents? I couldn't see myself wandering through an airport all alone.

The poster—spring break! Was my girl imitating the girl on the poster? The theories carved me up with jealousy. There had to be some way to find her. The most well-known athlete in Pond Bridge can't just disappear for a week.

The meme of me staring at her stomach popped into my head. "When he respects them abs." Twitter. Right then I stopped running halfway to her house and bolted straight home in the early morning darkness.

I tried my phone first, but I couldn't get the app to download. I erased precious games I'd been working on for months, but still nothing. The signal was too weak, and my phone was just too slow.

Next I tried the laptop. I paced back and forth during its startup cycle. Like a typical teenager it needed way too long to wake up. Finally, I clicked for a Wi-Fi signal, but they were all locked. I cussed a little too loud.

"You up?" I heard through Dad's door.

"No," I said, unplugging the laptop. I carried it outside as the battery immediately dropped to 40%. The screen glowed in the darkness as I aimed towards Willie's house. Still nothing. I looped around the yard holding the computer like a divining rod until finally, a signal. It was only one bar, and my battery was down to 31%, but I was online. I couldn't type while holding the laptop, so I crouched, and then finally sat in the dew of the grass. Ass soaked and arms trembling, the little blue Twitter bird finally appeared. It was calming and exciting at the same time. As if on cue, the morning birds began to sing from the trees.

Following directions, I entered my name and a handle: @3200RunnerGuy would do. Twitter prompted me to start following a bunch of celebrities, my favorite bands, comedians, and athletes, but none of them were of any interest. Search: *Angel Hayden*.

Just seeing her thumbnail picture made the itching on my legs disappear. The dampness I sat in no longer bothered me. There she was, mid-swing, probably belting a home run. I clicked on the page to unlock the enigma of where she'd been all week.

The first tweet was only hours old: *Goodbye Daytona #Springbreak* with a picture of a sunrise or sunset, I couldn't tell. Below was another picture of her. Her bare shoulders were a reddish brown tone glistening above a coral pink strapless sundress. The sun seemed to live in her cheeks and her smile glowed in front of the dark background.

How did I not think of this sooner? The Wi-Fi cut out before I scrolled. I clicked to reconnect and tapped on the monitor begging the universe for just a few more moments of information.

I wish it hadn't listened.

The next frame was a trio of pool pictures posted Tuesday evening. Before my eyes could absorb the glory of Angel in swimwear, another person intruded in the frame. He was touching her. My Angel—in a pool hanging on the shoulders of a man with a shaved head. Not a high school buddy. Not a guy who looked like he was a freshman in college. A grown-ass man. Twenty-two? Twenty-four? Her fingers squeezed the tattooed bicep as if she had captured him as her prey. His mouth was slightly open, and it sickened me to think how it probably just touched hers moments before. Angel, her soaked hair slicked back perfectly, had landed on him with an embrace that no one would've escaped. A green string on her bikini looked like it was about to come undone as she rested her entire chest on the back of his shoulder. Her ass, half out of the water, tightened in a perfect arc, and the flex in her thigh must have matched the intensity of when she scorched fastballs from the mound.

I wanted to puke. Instead I scrolled further. Another picture of the two of them, this time at least clothed, but standing at the front of a restaurant before being seated.

Caution: Battery is less than 10%.

That douchebag wore a Cincinnati ballcap and khaki shorts. His plain white shirt wasn't buttoned at the top so it revealed a patch of chest fur. Before I realized what I was doing, I had my hand under my arm measuring the tiny bit of hair I had grown there in the last couple of years.

The Wi-Fi cut out again, but I still had the image in front of me. I right-clicked to save and immediately cropped him out. Or most of him anyway. The image of Angel, in a white skirt and silver heels, grabbed me through the screen. Her top seemed to cut right down her side and I would've paid anything to see her spin. But she couldn't. It was a picture and there was still an invader's hand around her other shoulder.

Right then the screen went blank. I slammed the computer shut and fell back into the wet grass.

"Mark, what the hell are you doing?" Dad was standing in the back door.

"Can I get a better phone?"

16

Brian's spring break was a hundred times better than mine. I know because those were his exact words to me. During science, we got shushed enough times to risk detention. Brian insisted I visit his office during lunch. When I hesitated, he explained that Leah wouldn't be around for most of it because she actually had a new student to show around all day. To be on the safe side, I finished eating at Josh's table before trying to leave.

Mr. Mallett saw me on my way out of the cafeteria. "Going somewhere?"

"I've got an appointment with a student ambassador," I said. I didn't even break my stride. I felt his stare as I walked away. Maybe by the time I delivered my valedictorian speech at graduation next year, he'd see I wasn't a criminal.

True to his word, Brian was alone in his office. Leah's computer wasn't even on, and he offered me her chair to sit in. "It's okay. If she comes back all you have to do is get up."

Was this a trap? I settled in and faced him, but he was still turned to his desk. "Well, my whole thing is over," I said.

"Your thing?" He typed something at his computer.

"With Angel," I said. "She went on spring break with some guy. Some older guy. A man, I guess, and they're all over each other in the pictures."

"Ah, mining for pain," he said and turned around. "Stalking online is only going to end up with you finding things you don't want to. Especially with her."

"I wasn't stalking," I said. "You follow her on Twitter, what's the difference?"

"I'm just telling you, one minute you're going through her Twitter history, the next you're creeping through her bushes."

"Very funny." My face reddened. "You're a little smug today."

"I have an announcement myself," Brian said.

I guess my turn was over. I wished I could turn around and start typing on Leah's computer.

"Carissa and I made love last week." He said it like I owed him money from a bet.

"Congratulations?" I squirmed. "Is there a Hallmark card I'm supposed to get you or something?"

"Not yet, but soon."

"I'm not buying you a card." There wasn't a big enough firewall I could install into my imagination.

He closed his eyes. "I'm getting her a promise ring."

"Promise for what? Not to get her pregnant?"

"If you don't know what a promise ring is, you really are a child."

"I know what it is," I said. I mustered up everything I could. "I'm just kidding. Seriously, congratulations and everything."

"First I have to ask her to prom," he said.

The door opened slowly and Leah walked in. I hopped out of her chair as if she'd caught me going through her purse.

"Oh, that's okay," she said. "I just need to check something on my calendar."

I leaned against the door. "Well, we can finish this tonight," I said.

"Actually I need your help now," Brian said.

117

I nodded over at Leah. *Girl in the treehouse, abort mission!* Brian looked back at me, confused.

"Leah," he said, "what do guys typically do at this school for promposals?"

"For what?" She turned around and faced us. Her face was burnt and her freckles had multiplied to soft patches on her cheeks.

"Like, last year when Angel went to her junior prom, how'd the guy ask her?"

"She went with friends."

"Nobody asked her?" Brian looked up at me, but I suddenly felt the need to count the tiny holes in the ceiling panels.

"She's never been asked to a dance," Leah said. A pin dropped a hallway over. "Neither of us have."

Brian was still glaring at me, but I continued to lean on the door with my sweaty hands behind my back. "Well, maybe a card would do," Brian said. "I bought Carissa this stuffed frog on our trip, but I haven't given it to her yet." He reached down to a pile of stuff near his desk and started digging through a plastic bag. His shirt was untucked and half his crack was showing. This repelled Leah enough to turn back to her computer screen.

"Here 'tis," he said. He held up a cheap stuffed animal frog. "It's kind of an inside joke between Carissa and me. See, during vacation we were—" I gave a sideways nod. "I'll have to explain it later."

"So yeah, I'll help you tonight," I said, ready to eject from this cube of awkward.

"Let's just do it now," he said. He scooted back from his computer where a blank screen held a blinking cursor.

"Fine, get up," I said. His seat was so warm I thought I was going to stick to it. I thought for a moment, listed some words that rhymed with frog and typed some lines so ridiculous I thought it would cause another fight. If nothing else, it would make Leah laugh.

Brian replaced me in his seat and cleared his throat. Leah paused her typing.

"You're the beauty my eyes need to see in a morning so thick with fog. Please go to prom with me, my sweet princess, and I'll be the happiest frog."

Brian clapped his hands together in a hard smack then pumped his fist with a "Yes!" He got up out of his chair and bear-hugged me off of my feet. I felt a hint of the rib pain Katy had caused weeks ago. He repeated his thanks and slaps on the back until I couldn't take it anymore.

I exited the office to a cooler hallway. Through the door I could hear him reciting it over and over. I felt joy, though somewhat mild, from making him that happy. Maybe we'd get the friendship back on track. Despite the ruckus he had created, the one thing that stuck out to me after he'd read it—and I'm not even sure if it happened—but I could have sworn I'd heard Leah let out a little "Aww."

***

Brian rewarded me with rides to school the rest of the week. It allowed me to avoid Katy in the morning and get to school much earlier. The downside was that the next morning I had to hear more details about sex—or lovemaking, as he called it—than I ever needed to hear. Even more annoying, Brian felt the need to call Carissa so they could fight over who loved whom more. He used Bluetooth, so her voice echoed through four different speakers.

I continued to check Angel's Twitter whenever I could. The school computers blocked the site, but at night after Dad went to bed, I'd charge up the computer and signal-search my way through the yard until it connected. Every so often she'd include a spring break picture, though none with the guy she'd been clinging to in the pool. I saved every picture of her in a folder so I could look at them even without a signal.

My new favorite was an image of her lying along the shore. She was on her side with her hip gently pressed into the sand and her legs stretching forever. Her hair was still wet and pulled straight behind her. Without sunglasses her squint paired up beautifully with her smile. Her hand pointed to the shells, dozens of them, that she had arranged just out of the reach of each wave. They spelled out "Daytona."

When I saw her one morning, she was getting help from Mr. Bates. I walked into his room for first hour to this pleasant surprise. "Mark, you think you could help her?"

I dug through my pocket for a piece of gum while he put the monster-sized equation on the whiteboard. Angel's eyes were frustrated, nothing like the sparkling blue crystals I'd captured from Twitter. Math can do that to people, I suppose.

"Sorry, it just pisses me off when I don't get something on the first try," she said, standing up next to me. Her black gym shorts hung down to her knees, and her t-shirt was at least two sizes larger than it needed to be.

I picked up the red marker, but then set it down. Green would be more gentle. She took it from me with her eyes still scanning the problem. I chewed as much mint as I could from my gum and suggested where to begin. I must have grown a little because she didn't feel quite as towering.

Mr. Bates sat at his desk. He leaned back in his office chair. All he was missing was a footstool.

With each step of the problem, her tone improved. "Like this?" she would ask. If she started to make a mistake, I would twist my head. "No, oops, shit. . ." and she'd wipe the error off with the blade of her hand.

Her confidence grew. My confidence grew. Mr. Bates's smile grew.

"Last step," he announced. My classmates started to enter the room for first hour. Angel looked up to the clock and twisted the marker in her hand. All she had to do was divide one last part, but she didn't see it. Her brain was doing somersaults as her face twisted.

I pressed up on my toes and whispered in her ear. "Divide that last part." Shampoo, conditioner, body wash, maybe even some sweat, and whatever else girls wear, it all intoxicated me.

"Like this," she said completing the equation. Mr. Bates nodded as she celebrated with arms raised. She high-fived a girl in the front row who didn't seem to know her, and ran out into the hallway. "I don't suck at calculus!" She rushed back in, put on her backpack and grabbed both my shoulders. *Not here! Please!*

"I owe you one," she said and then hugged me so hard my back cracked. "I got an idea." I stood there bracing myself for more, but she left the room as the bell rang.

I stepped back and stared at the problem. It should be documented as an early relic to our relationship. Mr. Bates was looking at it too. Angel's handwriting sloped downward and the smudges illustrated all the hard work.

I looked at my teacher. "This isn't right, is it?"

"Not even close," he said.

17

That afternoon we had a track meet at Pineville. I assumed every guy on their team was the one who'd hosted the party Angel attended the night she saved me from Katy. Before I finished my warm-up laps, I changed my mind. Not one runner looked much older than me. Their freshmen ran around playing ultimate frisbee instead of getting ready. My fantasy of smoking a fellow suitor of Angel disappeared long before my race.

Josh won the 800, and I beat the field by at least half a lap in the 3200 with a PR of 10:56. Turns out not running eight miles the day before a race is highly beneficial. Katy still yelled for me for all eight laps. Most of those cheers were actually demands that I ask her to prom. She promised she would say yes if I won the race. When I crossed the finish line, a scream like no other echoed all the way to Pond Bridge.

The time had changed for daylight savings, so there was a little more sunlight when our bus pulled into school that evening. I woke Josh up from his bus ride nap and asked for a ride to my house.

"I need to run in and get my calculus book first," I said as we got off the bus last.

"It's the second day back, you can't have a test already," he said as he climbed into a new Camaro from daddy's dealership.

"I just want to be ready in case anyone needs help with her homework." I scanned the parking lot, always aware of Katy's location now.

Josh's expression wrinkled for a moment. "I'm not used to you actively trying to score. Welcome to adolescence. The ladies have been waiting."

I slipped through the entrance near the gymnasium, letting the heavy door close behind me. Red exit signs glowed in the hallways, and the only sound was a custodian's buffer half a building away.

"Relax," I mumbled. When I was in second grade, I thought the principals lived at the school. This made me laugh a little. I got to my locker's hallway, but then went back to the previous row. One locker stood out from the rest. It was decorated in blue and green with white letters that spelled H-A-Y-D-E-N. An assortment of tiny palm trees and starfish stickers surrounded her name. The reminders of Daytona weren't going to disappear. The A was loose, so I pressed my thumb into it until the letter stuck against the clear tape.

Like everyone else, Angel didn't use a lock. I looked both ways and held my breath to listen. Even the buffer was silent.

If I was wasting my time with her, I had a right to know, didn't I? I needed to protect myself. I wasn't snooping; I was investigating. Everyone has a right to know certain things about someone. I wasn't sure what I could find. She could go through my locker if she wanted to, and I wouldn't care.

I opened the door gently, but the sound still seemed to echo throughout the building. Inside the door there was a taped photograph. It was the picture of a little girl, maybe seven, holding a bat. Her baggy uniform didn't fit anything but her smile. The pants and jersey were bright white with a baby blue stripe up the sides. Her hair was dark, even darker than Leah's, but didn't even reach to her shoulders. I looked closer. Impossible that Angel was ever that size.

A plain, faded yellow hoodie I'd seen her wear once or twice hung from the hook. I lifted it with the care of a surgeon and smelled it. First at the front, then inside by the tag. The scent placed me right back into her truck the night we went out. They say you can't consciously smell pheromones, but something in me triggered. Satisfied, I returned the sacred garb and closed the door. No harm done.

I hurried over to my locker still basking in the discovery. The soft feel of the sweatshirt stayed on my hands. I would master the rest of the calculus curriculum if that's what it took to spend more time with her.

When I opened my locker door, I almost jumped back. A conch shell sat on my books in the top section—a creamy, pink twisted jewel of the beach waited patiently for me to find it. Stuck to it was a small blue Post-It that said, "Ask me to prom!"

No hidden cameras. It wasn't a prank. I dropped the prize into my backpack and ran outside to Josh's car. The engine was running and he was almost in the grass as I got in.

"It's fine, Katy's gone," he said. "So is everyone else."

"Look at this." I held the shell out.

Much like me, Josh was confused at first until he read the note. "She must've found it during her trip." He picked it up and smelled it. "Yep, still ocean fresh."

I nodded.

"Now all you have to do is buck up and ask her."

My thoughts spun. "Yeah, I can think of something by this weekend."

"I wouldn't wait," he said. "Jefferson's still on the prowl. Do it tomorrow."

"Tomorrow?"

"The note says 'Ask me to prom.'" Josh sounded annoyed. "She gets her way by asking for what she wants."

She makes it *evident*, I thought. I continued to spin the shell in my hands as if it came with further instructions. Josh probably

124

relished my fear, but stayed quiet about it as long as he could. He slowed down as we entered Pond Bridge's border.

"You'd be her first, too."

"Really? I thought that—"

"Her first prom date, dummy. And trust me, you'll be rewarded."

What's the opposite of having the wind knocked out of you called? Whatever that is, that's what it felt like.

"Good luck trying to focus on calculus," Josh said as we pulled into my driveway.

"Damn."

"What?"

"I didn't even grab the book."

***

I can't recall an athletic event that neared the amount of nerves I carried that next day. *Buck up and be a man*, I repeated after every class. My hope was to see Angel in the hallway while no one else was around. She had a reputation for roaming, so I asked to use the restroom in each of my first four classes, taking the longest routes possible. A few of my peers inquired about my stomach issues, but lied and said I was texting my dad about something.

At lunch Josh reminded me that Angel's softball team had an away game. "Catch her while they're loading the bus after school." I didn't like the idea, but at least it let me put it off for a few hours. I'd still keep using my bathroom privileges.

Be a man.

The final bell rang and excuses climbed down my throat to swim with the butterflies. I could wait until tomorrow. I could leave a note in her locker. I could use Twitter or help from a friend, or. . . I could be a man.

I exited the building on my way to track practice. Maybe their bus had already left. That wouldn't be my fault. I walked around the corner to the loading zone and looked. Eight or nine girls on the softball team stood in a loose circle, and some were already on the bus. Their dark blue away jerseys made them look militant.

Angel appeared from the parking lot. Her cleats sounded louder on the asphalt, like they were made of silver or some new element that only superstars could wear.

I walked a little closer.

Be a man.

I already had the answers to this test, I just had to take it. What was so hard?

Angel and her team were whooping in some language only they seemed to comprehend. Different tones meant different things, I gathered. It sure as hell wasn't Spanish.

I got a little closer and she spotted me.

Be a man.

Be a man.

I waved her over like I had a secret to share. She straightened up and smiled. "Oh my gosh, he's so cute," she said. The rest of the circle quieted down as she approached.

Be a man. You don't want Jefferson to get her.

"What's up, boy?" she asked.

Man!

"Will you go to prom with me?" I heard myself say.

"Aww." She took a step back and covered her heart with both hands, like she was starting her pitcher's windup. This was where she would say she's flattered *but...* I braced myself for the worst.

"Of course I will."

I'm a man!

She turned back to her teammates. "I'm going to fucking prom!"

I laughed as they cheered, but then she put her arms around me, picked me up and swung me around I don't know how many times. Finally she let go and my feet returned to the ground, my world still spinning.

Angel ran back to her teammates where they celebrated like she had just crossed the plate after a walk-off home run.

I was a man. Still dizzy from being swung around, but a man. With a prom date.

I trotted up to the field house for practice. Katy stood at the door, a sphinx ready to attack.

"Excuse me," I said. "I need to get to the locker room for men. I am one."

"You weren't supposed to do that," she said and moved aside. For the first time she acted and even sounded normal.

I don't know why, but it scared me even more.

18

All morning I looked forward to telling Brian and Josh about my prom date. I debated how to spread the news and rehearsed it during my run. When I walked into the science lab they both showed me that it was already all over Twitter: *Going to prom with the boy with the most endurance. #stud*

One of her teammates had snapped a picture of Angel twirling me around in case there was any question as to who this "boy" was. Sure, she'd thrown a one-hit shutout and tied her own record of twenty-one strikeouts in a seven-inning game last night, but that meant nothing. Angel recorded shutouts all the time. I was her first prom date.

Josh opened the conversation. "You throw a party for your girl last night?"

The anatomy PowerPoint was already projected on the screen up front. I buried my face in my notebook and began copying.

"Yeah, she was hurting this morning," Brian said.

"Can I enjoy one day without being mocked?" I said.

"She almost puked on my car," Josh said.

"She's sick?" I asked. That would be my luck. I finally score a date and she comes down with a crippling illness. Would I get credit anyway? Would it be like a rainout in softball and be postponed to a later date? Maybe I could feed soup to her for the next month.

"It's called a hangover," Brian said. Mrs. Roberts shut the lights off and shushed the class.

The next slide was a diagram of the entire female reproductive system. "I should ask my girlfriend to help me study this," Josh said. He was so earnest somehow.

Brian's face was stone, but I cracked a little. This led to Josh spitting out a bigger laugh, which wasn't ignored.

"Mr. Harding?" the teacher said.

"Mr. Harding is my father." And a generous donor to Pond Bridge High School.

"Josh, is there something funny about this?"

"I'm sorry," said Saint Joshua. "We had a teacher," he looked at me, "was it in fifth or sixth grade, Mark?"

"Fifth," I said, trusting him.

"This teacher we had in fifth grade, and I won't repeat the name, but anyway—"

"The point?"

"The teacher said that the diagram of the female reproductive system looked like a moose. Antlers and everything."

The class laughed with an innocence to help us move on. Houdini escaped again.

"That image should make it less threatening to you," Brian said. I kept my face near my notebook.

My friend had a bad habit of whispering the words he was writing down, but today he did it louder than usual.

"Fall-op-ian," he spelled out over the scratches of his pencil, "tubes lead down to the u-ter-us."

"Stop it," I whispered.

"Wow, even textbook lady parts scare you?"

"It's getting pretty smuggy in here," I said. We copied the rest of the notes in silence.

We were assigned a worksheet to fill the last ten minutes of class. I rushed to fill the diagrams in while Josh drew in the body of a moose on his. His focus was impeccable as he carefully selected different colored pencils for the job. "So how about this, guys," he said, changing his mind from light to dark brown for the moose's body. "Since we're all going to prom, I'll see if I can host the pre-party. We can do pictures and bullshit out back."

"Actually I have some plans already with Carissa," Brian said. He began copying my answers.

"Just come over after that then. We'll wait for you, kinda. I mean, I'll be hammered, but we'll wait for you." He colored in a blue sky.

"I'm in," I said. "If it's okay with Angel, of course."

"My old man has a fully stocked bar in the basement," Josh said. "She'll be down for it."

I pictured her lining up shots and spilling liquor all over me.

"Sure, I can drive then," I said. "Think your dad would let us take one of those big SUVs?"

"Oh, we're going limo. No one's driving on prom night." Sure, of course. Only poor people drove themselves. "We can all crash there afterwards too."

Brian turned his head to watch me comprehend it all.

"Where will you be?" I asked him.

He looked over both shoulders like he was sharing a secret from his ancestors. "I'm going to give Carissa the promise ring."

That was not an easy laugh to stifle. Josh morphed into sincerity. "Oh, congrats. Got it all planned out and everything?"

"Just about," Brian said.

"I meant life," Josh said.

"I don't even know what suit I'm wearing," I said. "I don't think my old one fits."

"Suit?" Brian said. "Are you stupid? You don't wear a suit to prom, you wear a tux."

Josh joined in as the two of them hypothesized Angel's reaction to her date showing up in a suit.

"Well where do I buy one?"

Brian's forehead fell to the table. "You rent one. It's called a mall. And you need to find out what color of dress she's wearing to coordinate it."

So this is what it felt like to be the dumb kid. Brian went on and on about vests versus cummerbunds and the different styles of ties versus the classic look old men like his grandpa kept alive. "How do you not know any of this?"

All the while Josh nodded along. "Didn't your mom ever—shit, sorry," he said.

Brian's shoulders sank.

"Sorry, this is just all new to me," I said. Josh looked at the clock and started putting his colored pencils away. The bell rang a little louder than usual.

During lunch I got a text from Brian. *Tomorrow night, you, me, Carissa, and Angel are going to the Perry Mall.*

I knew there was a reason he was still my best friend.

It didn't just stop with a text. I got a lecture on the phone that night too. "You have to talk. Don't just sit there quietly."

"I know."

"And don't bring up Katy. Or the softball game we were at. Or what colleges are recruiting Angel."

"I know."

"And make sure you dress nice. Not church nice, but nicer than school."

"Okay."

"And we'll pick her up first, so be ready a little after seven. But if we're late, just sit tight.

"Got it."

"And don't be running around with that little rug rat neighbor of yours. You can't go on a date with grass stains."

"That it?"

"And I like your dad, but keep him inside. If you try and introduce him to her that'll feel premature and scare her."

"Scare her?" Angel wasn't afraid of anyone or anything, but there's no way I wanted Dad talking to her anyway.

"Just follow my example with Carissa. Obviously we have a very healthy relationship. Watch how I open doors, pay for things, and tell her how great she looks."

"I'll just echo everything you say as soon as you say it."

"I'm trying to help. Don't mock."

"Anything else?"

"How are you paying for your tux?"

"I'm publishing all this sage advice and selling it to boys all over the world."

Brian sighed.

"I'll talk to my dad about borrowing some money," I said.

"Get his credit card. Cash is childish and if you don't have enough you're screwed."

"I thought only the owner of a credit card could use it," I said. He seemed more nervous about this date than I did, so I had to razz him at least a little.

The conversation with Dad was concise, although compared to Brian's lecture, anything was. He told me that when it came to dating, he wanted me to have good experiences. "This is why I have you pack your lunch all year," he said.

Tears welled into my eyes, but just for a moment.

"As men, we're usually expected to pay for our first dates, especially if we do the asking out." Something about this statement bothered me. Not the paying part, but the way he included himself. Weird.

"Now, are you going to prom with Angel Hayden or the girl from the track meet who—"

"Dad, seriously?"

"What? You should give everyone a chance."

The horn on Brian's ride honked loud enough to make us both jump. "Son, your shirt has shoulder nipples from the hanger."

I sprinted back up to the bathroom and wet them down. When I got back to the living room, Dad inspected me again. "Now they're just wet spots."

I rubbed my shoulders hard enough to start a fire.

"Untuck your shirt and go with the brown shoes instead of your sneakers."

"Thanks, older sister I never had." He handed me the credit card as I rubbed my damp shoulders one last time.

I didn't recognize the vehicle Brian was driving. It was an older town car that seemed to stretch half the block. The outside was solid dark brown, like a candy bar, and the interior was burgundy leather. Grandpa must have come through for him again. That also explained the hospital-like smell on the inside.

The front seat was empty, so I climbed in and pulled the door shut with both hands. I exchanged hellos with both girls but didn't turn far enough around to make solid eye contact. Brian nodded mild approval. The back seat was in the middle of a conversation about one of Carissa's teammates who thought she was hot shit at a party last week because she screwed the JV coach at a neighboring school.

I waited for a gap in the gossip. "How was practice today?" I asked right as Carissa continued to dish about her right fielder.

Brian looked at me, his hands at ten and two on the wheel like a bus driver, and mouthed, "Speak up."

This time I turned all the way around. Angel wore some sort of black workout pants. They weren't yoga pants or sweats, but they stretched splendidly over the form of her long legs. The sweatshirt was the yellow one from her locker. It was zipped up to her neck.

Carissa had on jeans and a thick, bright orange sweater, like she was ready to go skiing. I guess if she crashed, someone would spot that sweater from miles away.

"How did practice go today?" I directed my question at Angel.

"We never practice Saturday," she said.

Carissa countered. "Really? Our bitch coach makes us get up at seven. . ." and on the girls went comparing squads.

"I tried," I said under my breath to Brian. We'd entered the outskirts of Perry by the time they finally stopped softball chat.

"Did Josh tell you about his pre-party?" Angel said.

"Works for me," I said.

I felt Angel place her hand on my right shoulder. I hoped that my shirt was dry.

"Pre-parties are cool," Carissa said. "Who's Josh?"

"Yeah, he invited us, but I planned something else," Brian said.

"You didn't ask me though. Maybe I prefer the pre-party," Carissa said.

Angel's thumb rubbed on my shoulder. My heart and everything else on my body took notice.

"Trust me, hun," Brian said. He was almost laughing, but she was not. "I've got slightly better plans for the two of us."

This was paradise. Smug Brian, self-proclaimed relationship king, was in battle while I sat back and watched. Angel continued to glide her thumb on my shoulder as if she could smother their tiff that way.

"I just think it would be nice to get a few drinks and maybe meet some people before we go to a loud dance."

"Just trust me," he said. It reminded me of a parent with a small child.

"I think you could've asked, is all." Or a married couple.

The left turn signal clicked forever as we waited on the light to give us a green arrow.

"Mark," Carissa said in a sweet tone. "Wouldn't you have consulted Angel before making plans?"

"Uh." I looked to Brian, but his eyes stayed on the light. Angel's thumb halted, but stayed on my shoulder.

"How long have you two been together?" I asked. The thumb resumed, only now further up my collar, petting the little hairs on the back of my neck.

"I wonder if he knows the answer to that," Carissa said. Brian didn't dignify the test with a response. I had no idea how mad she really was. What the hell was there to fight for?

"Good one," Angel whispered in my ear. I smelled the mint mixed with the breath she'd kissed me with on that notorious night after the game.

I contemplated reaching up and holding her hand on my shoulder, but we finally pulled into the lot of the mall. Brain parked two rows behind the nearest car and explained how his grandpa would kill him if a dent appeared.

He and Carissa mumbled apologies to each other while Angel leaned in. "Don't worry. They're just showing off because they've been together for so long. You'll see someday."

With her? My future flashed in scenes on the long walk to the entrance. Of course I would ask her about plans ahead of time. She'd be the one to make them anyway, and as long as she was with me, what did it matter? What was so hard about relationships anyway? Just agree, have fun, and make out. They aren't anything a future valedictorian can't figure out how to make work.

I would have taken her hand, but they were both in the pockets of her sweatshirt. Her zipper was still completely up to her chin. Disappointing.

Cars with loud stereos cruised by between families in minivans. Even in Perry, I wanted everyone to see me with Angel. As I scanned the lot for an audience, Brian walked a few steps ahead to get the door for everyone.

The girls thanked him while I received a glare instead. The night was starting to feel like my driver's license test all over again. Was he going to hold a clipboard and score me on it later?

We used the doors by the food court and walked only a few feet. We were in the way of everyone, but the other three were oblivious.

"Why don't you guys get your tuxes rented while we do some preliminary pricing?" Angel said. Hurt and relief at the same time.

"Half-hour?" Brian said.

"Meet back here," Carissa said and pecked Brian on the cheek. I looked to Angel, but she'd already hopped into a line to get a taco. That's my girl.

I had no idea what I was in for.

135

19

Brian didn't say much on our stroll over to Mr. Tuxedo. The place smelled funny, burnt leather maybe, and I felt foreign surrounded by so many other customers sporting South Perry t-shirts.

"I've never done this before," I told Brian.

"You'll be saying that a lot these next few weeks, I imagine," he said. It seemed to change his mood. He led me past the racks of sport coats and between the headless mannequins that lined the aisles. A salesman measured us, and I copied whatever Brian said until he insisted on choosing the classic bowtie style. The salesman winked at me when I selected the more recent trend. Our other discrepancy was color. Brian explained that Carissa wanted him to wear purple; I found a shade of bright blue that I liked.

"Did Angel tell you blue?"

"Yes," I lied. "It's ocean blue."

"We know she likes the ocean," Brian said. Another jab.

The process took much longer than expected. Shoes, pants, coat sizes—on and on it went until finally we were up at the cashier to pay. I thought there was a mistake or maybe he was joking when $120.78 popped up for my total.

"Is that right?" I looked at Brian.

He ignored me and bought some cufflinks at the counter so that his total ended up just under $160.

"So where are the tuxes?" I looked around.

"We pick them up the Friday before prom," he said. "Put your receipt in your wallet."

I took out my four one-dollar bills and folded Dad's credit card and my receipt inside them.

On the way back through the mall I asked, "Think we can grab some food too?" Four bucks wouldn't go far for mall food, but I could ring something else up on the card. We entered the food court, but the girls weren't there. My first thought was that they'd abandoned us. Women did that sort of thing in movies all the time. I took a free sample from a guy with a tray of toothpick meats. "This is amazing," I said.

"We're already four minutes late. It would be rude to keep the ladies waiting."

He said this as we stood in the exact spot we were supposed to meet. I failed to understand the logic. After shifting our weight two or three times, Brian texted Carissa.

"Back of Nordstrom," he read back.

"I thought we were meeting right here though?"

He dismissed me with a laugh, and we began the trek back to the other side of the mall. By the time we got there, the girls were leaving the store. "Too expensive," Angel said. "Onward."

I stood beside her as we went up the escalator. When I was little, Mom had always made me hold her hand on this one. We turned down a corridor of shops that I always considered just mall filler. Each store thumped with dance music and some of them were so dark my eyes needed time to adjust. Skinny women with ambiguous ages and heavy makeup zipped around asking if they could help us. The customers dug through sales racks with a laborious nature. Dresses, tops, and accessories I couldn't identify flew everywhere. Every few minutes someone would push by me with an "excuse me." It was like I had walked into a women's locker room with the way they sneered at my presence.

While Carissa disappeared into a dressing room to try something on, Angel wandered over to the counter. I watched her sniff a tiny perfume sample and then spray it on her neck. She smiled and sauntered towards me, even skipping the last few steps. "Smell," she said, leaning over. The tip of my nose grazed her neck. "What do you think?"

"I like it," I said, even though I was too nervous to think about it. "Let me smell again." She leaned forward, and I took my time. It could've been horse piss for all I cared. It was amazing though. A fresh aquatic scent grabbed me. Before that moment, I'd never really understood the allure of perfumes. They were always stinky little cards that popped out of magazines. Angel's made me a believer.

"It's called Ocean Bay," she said.

I noticed Brian evaluating my exchange from the corner of my eye.

Carissa reemerged from the dressing room. "Did you try it on?" Brian said.

"I did. It was awful. Let's go." Her pouting reminded me of Brian during a bad round of miniature golf.

After the third store, Angel found an armful of dresses she liked well enough to try on. The sales lady directed us over to the dressing rooms. Angel paused and glanced back over at Brian and Carissa. They were in the corner behind a clearance rack embracing for some reason.

"Want to know her biggest mistake today?" Angel said to me. I raised my eyebrows. Girls had to strategize too? "She didn't dress for the occasion of trying a dozen dresses on."

"What do you mean?" I asked.

Angel pushed apart the saloon-style door of the nearest dressing room and hung the collection of dresses on the wall. I started to turn away.

"Hey. This is what I mean." She kept one door ajar while the other hand unzipped her sweatshirt, exposing a strip of uninterrupted flesh from the center of her neck to her waist. She

138

let go of the door and turned away. It swung shut, leaving me with one or two quick peeps at her bare back before closing completely.

"Mother of pearl," I said. I collapsed in a nearby chair. Brian and Carissa returned from their slow dance.

"Going any better?" Brian asked.

"It's going good, I'd say. I'm doing—yeah, it's good."

"Okay, you ready?" Angel called out.

"Yeah." I was, but my voice wasn't. Of all the words to crack on. What I'd just witnessed must have ignited the final stage of puberty.

Angel pushed through the doors, stunning me in her dress. It shined a hundred shades of silver and seemed to move around every curve of her body like it was made of liquid. Without straps, her shoulders looked even more grand. She pulled her loose hair around her neck on the right.

"A little help," she said, turning around. Her back was exposed again. I stood there stupefied. "Mark, can you zip me up?"

"Oh, sure." My hands trembled as I reached for the tiny zipper between her shoulder blades. There was a thin tan line across her back. I took a quick glance at her ass, and then began my task. I avoided touching her skin because I could tell my hands were cold. Those damn nerves.

Right then Carissa stepped out in a light brown dress. Her bare feet thumped over to Brian. "Do you like it?"

He didn't. It was obvious. Her knees seemed to stick out and steal the attention away from the rest of her. She stood next to Angel. Day and night. Game, set, match.

"It's okay, but I don't think it highlights your best features," he said. "And with my purple tuxedo vest. . ."

Well played, Brian.

"Get a picture of us, so we can see," Carissa said.

Like I was drawing a six-shooter in the Old West, my phone was out, firing away as Angel posed. Carissa stood straight as Brian snapped a shot from the front and one from the side. Angel was already back into the dressing room.

"Mark?"

"Right here," I said.

"Gonna need your help again. Same issue." I waited just outside the door. "Are you there?" She pushed the door open. "In here."

I stepped into the dressing room, a portal from boyhood to manhood. Her pants and sweatshirt lay at my feet, both inside out. A large mirror reflected Angel next to me, my expression the definition of terrified.

"Aww, look at us. We're cute." She put her arm around me. My whole body must have been blushing. "Let's get a mirror selfie."

I fumbled my phone and it bounced off its rubber casing, which saved the stupid thing yet again.

"I'll get it," she said and reached down. "Wow, this is old school. Let's use mine." She dug into her sweatshirt pocket and pulled out the latest model of phone—which I still didn't have a number for. Her bright pink case had a 20 in glitter stickers on the back.

She pulled me next to her just as she had before I dropped my phone. I inhaled the perfume again and smiled. We both looked into the mirror.

"Perfect," she said. "This is getting tweeted." I stood there wondering if my job was done and stuck my thumbs in my pockets. Hers were typing in a flurry. This picture would certainly do more for my popularity than the meme from the cafeteria. She dropped her phone face-up back onto her sweatshirt.

"Oh yeah, the zipper," I said. *Calm down, boy.*

Her phone screen was already lighting up. I unzipped the top of her dress thinking about how many times I'd seen this same routine on smutty cable TV shows. Due to censorship it would always cut away at the best part.

"There ya go," I said. *Stop being so chummy.*

"Wow, look at all those likes pouring in," she said, picking up her phone.

I pictured Jefferson sitting somewhere by himself, buried in jealousy.

"Let's do one more selfie without the mirror this time," she said. Then she lowered her voice. "Just one for us." With her dress unzipped, she peeled off the top and covered her whole chest, barely, with her arm. My knees nearly buckled like when a friend kicks you from behind.

"Smile," she said and held the camera just above our faces. I was definitely smiling. I glanced at the mirror because you can't look straight into the sun. So much skin!

"Okay, I'll be out in a minute," she said. I slipped through the doors back into the universe I was familiar with.

Carissa was spinning for Brian in a peach dress. "That's the one," he said. "You, my lady, will be the belle of the ball."

Keep believing that, I thought. "And it goes with purple, right?" I realized I could talk with Carissa more easily now.

"Oh my!" I heard Angel say, still in her dressing room. She started laughing. "Probably not going to work for prom," she said.

The doors parted and Angel glided out in a crimson dress that would have gotten her banned from any Pond Bridge school function. It split all the way down the middle, exposing the same stretch of torso as the unzipped sweatshirt. She shifted her stance and a long leg appeared from the giant slit that didn't close until right below her hip.

I scratched the back of my head to prevent my eyeballs from popping out cartoon-style.

"Oh my gosh, you hooker," Carissa said, laughing. Brian's eyes shifted back and forth from Angel to me.

"Spin," I said. I twirled my index finger and she obeyed. Who the hell was I tonight? I couldn't tell which of us surprised Brian more, but the look on his face let me forgive his earlier cracks.

Carissa started snapping pictures on her phone, so I did the same. "Send me one of those," Angel said with her hair pulled above her head.

"Done," Carissa said.

"Here's a good one too," I said. "I don't have. . ."

Angel laughed. "So cute," she said, taking my phone. Her thumbs weren't as quick on my crappy screen. I looked at my new contact: "ANGEL, QUEEN OF THE WORLD" was finally added.

The Queen of the World changed back into her sweatshirt while Carissa bought the peach dress.

"Are you going with the silver one?" I asked over the door.

"No," she said. She emerged through the doors one last time in her black pants and yellow sweatshirt. "Tonight was just for fun anyway. I've got a dress from a while back that I never got to wear." She took my hand and squeezed. "And it'll knock your fucking socks off."

20

I woke up well before sunrise and got my morning run out of the way. No venturing to Edge Road. No need. But when I got to the gate of the cemetery, my legs told me to turn around and go home. I can't explain it, but I didn't feel like the same son who had been there just 24 hours ago. I wasn't her little boy anymore, and it probably made her sad.

I surprised Dad when I suggested to him that we go to church Sunday morning. He asked if I'd done something wrong. Not yet, I thought. I told him it just felt like we hadn't been in a while and it was the right thing to do. There aren't many Catholics in Pond Bridge, so it took a drive to Elk Falls to make the 9:15 start.

On our way home from Mass I told Dad I would work to pay back the credit card debt I'd run up. "Can I use it one more time?" He looked at me for an explanation.

"I want to get something for someone."

"A little vague," he said.

"Perfume for Angel."

He smiled. "I've been there. Don't go nuts."

Without my crew, the shop with the perfume felt twice as foreign. The music was cranked way too loud for a Sunday morning. Faint lighting and a low ceiling contributed to the atmosphere that apparently squeezed dollars out of teenagers. There were no windows, of course. I heard casinos are the same way so that guests never worry about what time it is.

I dodged a pack of middle-schoolers and found the perfume counter. It was near a cashier who had bright orange hair. She ignored me. Neon Carrot messed with hangers and checked her phone. I waited patiently as she rang up over $200 of clothing for a girl who might have been 12.

"Excuse me," I said and then repeated myself.

"Are you finding everything okay?" she asked, and began folding some returns. I could have held up a middle finger and she wouldn't have noticed. I almost did.

Was it a sign from the universe? Maybe it meant I shouldn't make the purchase. It was a lot of money. Besides, Angel liked me already.

Be a man.

I cleared my throat and gave my voice a brief sound check to make sure it didn't crack. "I want to buy some perfume for my girlfriend."

My girlfriend. That must be what people feel like the first time they get to attach "Doctor" to their name.

"Of course. Do you know which one?"

"Ocean something?" Not quite knowing would seem cooler.

"Ocean Bay? We have that right over here." Her heels clicked against the floor. "There's the travel size for $68, and then the gift package for $109. The travel size is just an ounce and a half, but the gift size of 4.3 ounces and comes with a lotion, a silver key chain, and of course the designer bottle." She reached under the counter. "I'll give you a moment to check it all out."

I barely listened to the spiel about the $109 rip-off. Ha! She didn't know who she was dealing with. I wasn't going to spend $41 more dollars, the equivalent of several weeks of paying Dad back, on a couple more ounces and add-ons.

Then I saw the bottle. She set it down on the counter next to the lotion. It was the shape of a shell. The pink translucent reflections danced off the shape. Someday we would vacation on a beach together. If she's the one, what did that little amount of money matter?

What did anything else matter? Whether it happened at prom, six months from now, or years from now? It was still going to happen, so why wait? I ignored the melody from the church organ that still rang in my head.

"I'll take the package," I said, swiping another deep cut into dad's credit limit. Maybe he'd understand. Maybe he already understood. Maybe he'd kill me. It didn't matter.

The risk was worth the reward.

***

With prom still almost two weeks away, Angel and I didn't see each other during school very often. I recalled Josh's mantra: "Once you lock a girl in for a date, the only thing you can do is screw it up by smothering."

I stuck to texting Angel once a day. Twice she even texted me first. We developed our own hieroglyphics with emojis. I used a beach theme when I could. That way she would learn to associate it with me and me only.

Each night I logged our interactions on a spreadsheet. Conversations, Twitter likes and replies, the peck on the cheek Tuesday after lunch, and of course the 30 different smiley faces.

Katy ceased her school spectacles. Students still harassed me about her every day, but it seemed playful now. By the second track meet that week, she was no longer screaming her brains out for all eight of my laps. I take a lot of credit for that because of what happened before practice on Wednesday.

She waited by the fieldhouse again, arms folded and huffing.

"What is it this time?" I asked.

"You asked out the wrong girl to prom. And after all we've done."

Make it évident. Who cares if it's mean? I pulled out my phone and thumbed my way through the Angel pictures.

"Okay, it's area code 419—" she began reciting.

"I'm pretty sure I asked the right girl. Woman, actually." I held up my favorite shot of Angel in the crimson dress. Image 034 captured her at her best angles.

Katy gave one last huff, strong enough to blow down a house made of sticks, and possibly bricks, before stomping away. "He just doesn't get it!" she yelled.

I saw a few heads turn from the parking lot. Thank you.

I was on fire all week, but Brian's fortunes were plummeting. By Thursday morning in science, he couldn't hide his panic. Carissa had told him she was as sick as a dog. "I tried to bring her some flowers and orange juice, but she said she didn't want me to get sick too." He looked at his open palms.

"Flowers and orange juice," Josh mumbled, and for some reason it was the funniest thing I've ever heard. I bit the tip of my tongue and mashed my hands into my face. If Josh and I made eye contact we would've laughed so hard Mr. Mallett would have heard us from his cave. I turned my focus back to my worksheet, but just when I thought the spell was over, it picked up again. Tears streamed from my eyes, and I choked back the spasm as best as I could.

"You're in a good mood, I guess," Brian said. He moved my hand so he could see my answer for number two.

I wiped the tears from my face. "Yep, life is good." *Flowers and orange juice?*

"What should we do Friday night?" He rubbed the scruff on his chin. "Well, depending on if the quarantine for Carissa is lifted."

Josh shot me a smirk. I was thinking the same thing.

"I'm going to try and take Angel out."

"Do or do not—" Brian began.

"I know, I know."

"Isn't there the post-season basketball party?" Josh asked.

There was, but an unwritten rule said it was varsity only, unless you were a really popular underclassman. "I'd rather spend time with Angel," I said.

"Than with your best friend?" Brian asked.

"Really?" I pulled my phone out right then. Mrs. Roberts wasn't looking so I lap-texted Angel.

You free Friday night?

Kinda. Yes, she texted back in record time.

It showed she was typing more. Amazing.

Jean's diner at 7?

I used the smiley face with hearts for eyes to confirm.

"Well?" Brian asked.

"I have plans."

Josh clapped. "Flowers and orange juice, my boy. Flowers and orange juice."

21

Jean's Diner was one of those landmarks I noticed every time I went to the mall, but it felt more like scenery. I think Dad commented about it being overpriced when I was younger and that contributed to the negative connotation. I didn't mention that I'd be using his credit card there. One last time in the name of dating. It was also in the name of dating that I showed up a half hour early and sat in my car until seven. Still no sign of the blue truck, but I went in anyway.

The diner smelled like coffee and grease, and the decorations on the walls were from one of those decades when people still said words like *swell* and *golly gee*. Half of the tables were occupied by twenty-somethings or other teens. A family with a screaming toddler sat in the corner.

A hostess with a grown-up face but a child-like body approached. "Just one tonight?"

"Two please. My girlfriend's late."

"Sounds like a call for a celebration," she said and laughed. "Sorry, I'm kidding. That's not funny."

I didn't get it anyway. She led me to a table on the side. "I'll sit you here so you can watch for her at the door." I sensed she didn't believe me.

I slid into the booth and leaned against the wall, hiding the gift bag on my lap. After tonight I would stop feeling crazy and insecure about our relationship. The perfume would express how I felt about her. She would think of me every time she put it on. We could develop some sort of routine where I would smell it and kiss her.

The diner grew busier. I read over the entire menu three times. Dad was right about the prices. Maybe she would only order a shake since they didn't have tacos.

They say smokers get a tingle of anticipation right before they light a cigarette because their body wants one so badly. I felt that same tingle every time I saw her. I looked up right as Angel entered. She always overwhelmed her surroundings. I bet people knew who she was. She had on another pair of black pants and a tight white V-neck that would challenge me—or anyone, really—to sustain eye-contact. I couldn't believe she was mine. In one hand she held two bags, black and pink, that must have come from the mall. Her other hand was texting.

The hostess looked like a munchkin in comparison. "I think your boyfriend is already here," she said. Angel let out a little laugh, and I'm not sure, but I think I saw her head shake no. I deflated a bit, then returned to memorizing the menu.

"Hey, stud," she said, sitting down across from me.

"Hi, Angel." Just as I rehearsed, but then my brain screamed a hundred other orders at once. *Tell her she looks beautiful. Ask her how her day was. Give her the perfume. Say something interesting!*

"Sorry I'm late. Had to pick up a few more things for next week."

"That's okay. I haven't been here very long either." I glanced up at the clock with the neon sign border. It was twenty after seven. "When's your next game?"

149

Her phone buzzed on the table. "Just a sec." Her thumbs attacked the screen. "Group text with my sister and. . ." She sent it and set the phone back on the table.

"We have an invitational meet tomorrow morning," I said. "It's a bit of a drive, but if you want to go. . ."

"Oh, we play Rigmore tomorrow morning."

"That's a pretty big matchup, right?" I'd rather watch that than run in my stupid meet.

"Number three in the state. They have a girl going to Arizona next year, plus a few others who signed division one."

"You can beat 'em though, right?"

"Sure," she said and gave me a cocky nod. Her phone buzzed again. This time her reply took longer. "Stupid Todd," she said. I waited to hear who the hell Todd was, but the server parked by our table.

Angel flipped open a menu. "I'm starving, but I'm not sure what I want yet. You go first."

"I'll have the waffles and a small chocolate shake," I said. Just over ten bucks for my half.

"I would like," she flipped the menu over twice, "the grilled cheese supreme and a Coke."

Just over twenty. I could cover that with my own savings.

"And a double order of fries."

"Regular, curly, or sweet potato?" the server asked. "The last two are two bucks extra."

"Oh, gotta go curly, of course."

Of course.

"And do you have banana shakes?" She finally closed the menu. The server nodded.

"A large, please."

She returned her eyes to me. Her face only had a little makeup and I wondered if now was when I should tell her she looked beautiful.

"So how was the mall?"

"Oh, a little crowded. I had to pick up some intimates." She made a silly face and hissed out the s. I was pretty sure I knew what intimates were. My heart revved up.

"I got you something the other day," I said and lifted the red gift bag onto the table. I prayed that she didn't notice the Christmas design on the side.

"Mark!" It felt like a kiss when she said my name. "You didn't have to get me anything." Her shoulders slouched. "I didn't get anything for you." Then she peeked into the pink bag. "Well, actually I did, I guess."

The headline will read, *"Local Pitcher Dissolves Junior Boy into a Fine Powder After His First Prom Experience."*

She removed the box from the bag which I swiped back down to my lap. Her eyes grew as she realized what it was. "That perfume. I love it!"

"Look at the bottle," I said.

Her thumb opened the box and she carefully removed the bottle. "A shell," I said.

"Wow, cool." The connection would click. It had to. Our family coat of arms would be a shell.

Angel sprayed her wrist and then wiped it against the side of her neck. Her phone buzzed on the table again.

"Sorry, this stupid friend of mine." She pretended to be upset at the interruption. "So in a last-ditch effort to get Leah a prom date, she's taking this guy we've known forever."

Poor Leah, I thought.

"His name's Todd and our families are good friends. My dad works with his dad, our moms know each other, we vacation together and all that."

The waitress set our shakes down. Mine looked like something from the kids menu, a thick red foot long straw barely staying in a tiny plastic cup. Angel's shake came in a heavy glass. There was a cherry on top. She got the metal container with bonus shake too.

I sucked a little through my straw, but since the word "vacation" came up, my stomach wasn't interested anymore. "So where does Todd go to school?" I put my mouth back on the straw to disguise my frown.

She picked up the cherry and plucked it off the stem. It disappeared behind her lips. "Oh, he's a Cincinnati Bearcat."

Just like the hat in the picture.

"And he's going to our prom?" I wanted to laugh, but it's impossible when your heart is being kicked around.

She shrugged and stirred her shake. "Like I said, he's a close family friend, so. . ."

Close. The word polluted my confidence like venom. Her phone buzzed again. I leaned back in the booth. What would it take to make her mine and mine only?

"I. Don't. Know." She vocalized her text. "Josh said Leah and Todd could come over too, so we're trying to plan what time. I'll just meet you there I guess."

"I'll just meet you there I guess" is the least romantic phrase in the English language. It did, however, spare me from having to pick her up at her house where I'm sure her parents would be ready to interview me.

I pictured Mr. Hayden saying, "Oh, that's the boy who runs past our home at all hours of the morning."

I tried to get the conversation back. "So I thought you'd like the bottle because it's a shell, and you know."

"I do miss the beach," she said. "Thank you again. Oh, and there's lotion and a keychain too?"

Angel investigated the rest of the contents as I reevaluated my entire existence. If the whole shell motif didn't trigger a connection, was it possible that it hadn't even been from her? Had I surprised Angel when I asked her to prom?

I replayed the moment in my head. I'd walked across a tightrope a hundred feet in the air thinking there was a safety net below me. Like the man I was.

And then Katy was upset and told me *I asked the wrong girl!*

Oh no.

All those nights I'd spent with the shell right next to me in bed, and it was Katy's. I'd be lucky if it wasn't bugged. No wonder she was so defeated.

I looked over at Angel as she rubbed a dab of lotion just above her cleavage. "Wanna smell?" she laughed. I smiled, unable to answer. "Later on then."

I needed a timeout to comprehend everything. Weeks ago I hadn't had the courage to talk to this woman. This all-state, high school sports celebrity. This "Queen of the World." And because of an insane girl named Katy getting me a detention, I had the opportunity to go where. . . I guess several men have gone before.

Our food showed up shortly after that. Angel asked me about track with the usual questions. "How do you run that far? Is it fun? Do you usually win?" I told her about my morning routine running around town, and mentioned Mr. Bates as a great coach. We agreed on how worthless calculus was before she asked me why I was taking it as a junior. I tried to answer without sounding like a nerd, and focused on guiding the conversation back to track.

"So, like, what do you think about while you're running all those miles?" she asked. She dipped her fries into the last of the ketchup on her plate.

I was ready for this one. A lot of people ask it. Usually I think about video games, or my mom, or random childhood memories. "Lately, I've been thinking about you." I watched her face melt into an expression that didn't want to cry, but did. *Lender, you romantic bastard.*

She moved over to my side of the booth and kissed me on the cheek. She wrapped her arm around me and sobbed a bit, trying to contain herself. "That's the sweetest thing anyone's ever said to me."

Really? I had much better material than that. I hadn't even begun to express my potential sweetness. Maybe that stupid frog poem I wrote for Brian had been gold after all. I should start charging him more.

153

Angel's warmth covered my side. She sniffed again and wiped her face with a napkin and then laughed. "Sorry, I'm a hormonal mess I guess."

I whispered, "That's okay."

"It could work out in your favor very soon."

"Check, please," I said. "Too bad we both have events tomorrow. Our bus leaves bright and early at 7:30."

"Ours doesn't leave until seven. Aren't you going to stop by Andy's? You played basketball, right?" She wiped her face one last time and returned to her side of the booth.

"I wasn't going to. They're probably already drunk, and I have to get up early, plus—" Plus, Jefferson won't even let me sit at his lunch table, let alone attend a party he's at.

"Oh," she said. "I should skip it too since I pitch tomorrow."

I exhaled.

"Maybe I'll just run in real quick and say hi. Are you going to finish your waffles?"

I slid my plate across the table and she finished up. I cringed at the check. It reminded me of getting a test back I knew I had bombed. It would take the first month of my summer job to pay Dad back.

Angel thanked me for dinner, and I walked her out to her truck. "Prom's going to be so much fun," she said, leaning against her door. She put my gift in one of her bags and thanked me again. I nodded and went to kiss her. She reciprocated and put her arms around me. Minutes? Hours? No idea. We were that couple making out in the parking lot of a diner.

Finally she released me. "Sure you don't wanna swing by the party?"

"I'd better not." There was no point. I could only screw it up from here.

"Oh. Well good luck at your race tomorrow."

"And you pitch me another two-hit shutout," I said.

Her smile looked fake.

154

22

Dad's forehead grew another wrinkle when I told him I was going to bed so early. He pointed out that the Indians game was only in the sixth inning. "Josh is picking me up at 6:45 tomorrow morning," I said.

An eternity later I was still awake. I heard the familiar piano from the theme song from reruns of *The Office* on the other side of my door. I forced my eyes closed and thought about my race. I thought about video games and the last basketball season and a fifth-grade spelling bee and a field trip our freshman year and my mother. What would she say about Angel?

"I've just heard something about that girl. She's a drinker. You aren't into that, are you?" I tried to come up with a list of reasons for Mom to like her, but none sounded logical. Dad certainly didn't need convincing. I flipped my pillow over and adjusted my sheets.

A famous author named Alexandre Dumas, whom I paraphrased a report on once, once wrote: "Never did a man deeply in love allow the clocks to go on peacefully." I'd stuck the quote on a poster for my project, not understanding it at all. Now it echoed and laughed at my illusions of slumber.

My imagination started painting pictures of the party I'd passed on. Jefferson was sprawled out next to Angel on a couch. One of

155

their heads, probably his, would tilt ever so slowly onto a nearby shoulder. A hand would touch an elbow, then move down to the fingers. Angel's thumb, which had strummed my neck, would find its way to his forearm and realize how much more muscular he was than me. The rest of the party would be a chaotic mess of broken lamps, beer bongs, and loud music. The two of them, unnoticed, could slip into an isolated guest room.

Which could work out for you later, she had told me. It was later and I was eight blocks away, curled up in my twin-size bed while she was under the same roof as Jefferson and the rest of the team of perverts. I stood on my bed. With my head inches away from the ceiling, I made a decision. I had to go get her.

Fully dressed now, I walked into the living room. The light above the kitchen sink and the television were enough to see Dad still lying on the couch.

"Sneaking out?" he asked.

"Yes."

"Where to?"

"Andy's house. There's a basketball party and I want to make sure Angel gets home okay."

"You didn't go with her?" I looked at the clock above the mantle. It was a few minutes before midnight. "She's there with the guys, huh?"

I appreciated his concern, but it only made me feel dumber. "I have a meet tomorrow, and wanted to get some extra sleep, but—"

"Keys are on my dresser," he said. "Pick up some milk on the way—never mind. Just be safe."

"I promise I won't be drinking."

"I meant the other thing." The television lit up Dad's face for a brief moment.

"What else would be danger—oh," I said. "Don't worry," I laughed.

"I'm not worried about whether you do that or not, I'm just telling you to be safe if you do."

I froze as the TV continued to play with the lighting on our faces. "Wouldn't it be wrong either way?" I asked.

He waited until the TV was darker again. "It's a part of life. It certainly doesn't define a person, but it's part of it."

He probably didn't see my nod. In fact, I don't think I gave him one.

***

Andy lived a block and a half from Jefferson. It's like everyone on that street was bred to become a tall asshole. I circled the area until I spotted the rusty blue truck. It was parallel parked facing the wrong way, but when all ten of the Pond Bridge police force are softball fans, it doesn't matter.

I walked down the center of the street listening for loud music, but there wasn't any. Just the same dogs who always barked at me in the morning. A cherry of a cigarette glowed from the porch. I crossed under a street light and into the driveway.

"Lender, that you?"

"Yeah."

"'Bout time. Beer's inside if there's any left."

I walked up the stairs two at a time to the porch. Jefferson greeted me with a fist bump and then flicked the smoky butt into the grass. He wavered a bit, but got the door for me. Weird.

Inside, a giant couch bent around the room. Just like in my living room, the television provided most of the light. Legs and arms were twisted among the familiar faces. It looked like a game of Twister had crashed onto the couch. I scanned the faces for Angel. A few sober-enough nods acknowledged me, but one face ducked away. Whoever it was, she felt the need to bury their identity against the chest of our point guard. She didn't have Angel's legs, so I wasn't worried.

I walked into the kitchen area. A soft glow shone from above the cabinets. The table held a mix of empty bottles and cans. A snapped vape was in two pieces on the counter. I decided to check back on the living room situation and figure out who was hiding. I tiptoed towards the dark room and then casually entered.

157

I recognized her immediately. "Hey, Carissa." Busted! "You know where Angel is?"

She swore under her breath. "Upstairs, I think."

"Just stay out of the first two rooms," Andy's voice said from somewhere in the tangled mess.

I walked in front of the TV to get to the stairs. "Glad you're feeling better," I said. She covered her face like a toddler. "I won't say anything to Brian. But you should probably be honest with him soon, because—"

"I know," she said.

I walked up the carpeted steps. There were twice as many as in my house, and they weren't nearly as steep or noisy. Even with a party of teenagers, the home still smelled like expensive candles. The hallway was immaculate too. The third room on the right was open, so I started my investigation there. A cellphone glowed. Whatever was happening inside would decide how much I really meant to her.

"Angel?"

"Who's there?"

I walked in and almost stumbled on her legs. "Hey, I made it after all." I waited as my eyes got used to the darkness.

"Come sit with me," she said. She lay on her back.

I banged my head against something plastic hanging from the ceiling.

"Watch out for that mobile," she said. "I did the same thing."

"Are we in a nursery?"

"I guess so. That or Andy has some growing up to do." She laughed too hard at this, and when I rested my head next to hers I could smell why. A lot of those empty bottles downstairs were hers.

"Andy's dad is cool," she said.

"Is he here?"

"No, no. He's in Vegas with his girlfriend and their daughter. Or son, shit I don't know, whoever sleeps in this closet."

"I can't imagine my dad dating. Or having a baby daughter."

"Or letting you host a party," she said. We both laughed a little, then it got quiet again.

"Mark, are your parents divorced?" Her phone buzzed. "This stupid thing." She chucked it towards the door where it bounced and hit the wall. "Sorry about that. I forget what I said."

"That's okay." I listened to her breath for a few moments. "You still smell really good—"

"Oh I remember now. Are your parents still together?"

I debated throwing my phone. Or lying. Or just kissing her. But if she was going to be my girlfriend, she needed to know.

"My mom passed away a couple years ago."

"What?" She sat up. "Oh my God, that's right. I remember now."

"Yeah, it's just one of those things." One of those things I need to mention at a better time.

"I'm so sorry. How did I not remember that?"

"Angel, it's okay." I loved saying her name. I sat up next to her and felt around on the carpet until I found her hand. I put mine on top of it. We stayed motionless for another minute.

"You're like the best person I know," she said. Her phone buzzed again. It was even louder vibrating against the wall. "You're like a. . ."

Don't say brother. Don't say brother.

She didn't say brother. Instead, she used her foot to kick the door closed. Blind in the darkness, I was pushed onto my back again and she was on top of me.

Was this going to be how it happened? Sympathy sex for having a dead mom from an intoxicated Angel? She sealed her mouth onto mine, and I learned that I didn't like the taste of whatever hard cider had transformed her into this condition.

She pulled my shirt up halfway, but I was too scared to pull it off the rest of the way. That's when I felt her bare stomach against mine. A small stinging sensation struck my lower abdomen. "Oww," slipped out.

159

"Sorry," she said. "I was gonna wait until prom to show you, but I got the piercing." Then she started whispering. "Here. Feel it."

She pulled my hands against her stomach. It was soft around the sharp stud of whatever stone decorated her belly button. Her shirt was off, there was no mistake.

I'd just let it happen. It was time to outgrow daily visits to the cemetery anyway. Mom would want me to be happy in love. I was sick of feeling guilty about everything. Fuck it.

She guided my hands up her bare sides. I tried to recall every YouTube video I'd watched about removing bras.

Then the door suddenly swung open.

Angel's body—amazing, by the way—eclipsed the figure, who'd apparently never heard of knocking.

Straddling me, Angel turned around. "What the fuck, Leah?"

"Dad's outside in his truck. The UCLA scouts called and said they're going to your game tomorrow. Put your clothes on and let's go."

Moments later I was alone and on my back in some little kid's nursery.

That next morning I ran my worst race in three years.

Angel threw a perfect game and was offered a full ride to UCLA.

Come Monday I planned on holding her hand through the middle of the hallways.

Except she didn't come to school.

She was absent Tuesday too.

23

Just stupid personal stuff, is all she revealed through texts.

Brian and I got to school early and stood in the cafeteria to buy our prom tickets. Other couples held hands, kissed ears, and a few even embraced in a silent slow-dance. Mr. Mallett walked up and down the lengthy line like an armed guard at a bank, tapping the shoulders of the couples who got too passionate.

They hadn't announced the location of prom until that week: Elk Falls. Far enough so that it wasn't in our back yards, but close enough not to scare all of the designated drivers away. Student council rented Ballroom B of the town's outdated convention center for Saturday night's festivities. Our budget couldn't even secure Ballroom A.

"I need a small favor," I said to my best friend.

"I thought you said your dad loaned you the cash for this." He pulled out his wallet mobster-style.

"That's not it. Angel's been out all week."

"Carissa was sick last week, but she recovered."

A miracle! And without flowers and orange juice.

"Angel's not sick, she just won't say where she is."

"So what's the problem?" We moved a little closer to the stage area where weeks before my humiliation had been on display.

"Could you just maybe bring it up to Leah? See what she says?"

He rolled his eyes and shook his head. "Just come back to the office and ask her yourself."

"I don't know. I don't think she likes me very much. Probably just a sister thing, right?" A few spots back in line, Katy stood with a handful of cash. Her Marky Radar was turned off for once.

"I'd consider Carissa's sister a good friend. You should work towards that." Mr. Pompous had never once brought up Carissa's sister.

"When are you giving her the promise ring?"

"Shh!" He smacked my arm. "Only you and Josh know about that."

I looked around for anyone who could possibly give a shit. Katy saw me, but stayed quiet.

"That's weird," I said. "You-know-who is behind us, and she's not screaming my name."

Brian turned but didn't acknowledge her. "Once I pick Carissa up, there's a nearby park we're getting pictures at. I'll do it then." Carissa had three full days to tell him the truth. "Where are you and Angel getting your pictures at?"

"Can't we just do that as we get to prom?"

His fingers slid down his face. "Okay, go on the internet and look up Prom 101 or something."

"Seriously, is there something wrong with Katy? She's not making a scene or anything."

"If I didn't know any better, I'd say you're upset about it or something." Brian looked straight over my head as he talked.

"Brian, there's something. . ." Would it hurt him more coming from me or Carissa? "Never mind."

We didn't say anything else until it was our turn to purchase. Brian placed a crisp fifty-dollar bill on the table and received his green couples' ticket.

"One please," I said.

"Are you serious? You're not buying hers?"

"She told me not to." I pulled out my phone to show him the text from a week ago. "See? It says *Please let me buy my ticket.* There's even a little heart next to it."

"That's not a good sign," he said.

"Trust me. I'm in."

"Oh yeah? How do you know?"

"I know a lot more than you think." I set down three fives and ten one-dollar bills and received my ticket.

***

After school I caught Angel as her team loaded the bus to another game.

"You feeling better?" I asked.

She looked over my head the same way Brian had. "Not really," she said. We embraced but she put her cheek against mine so I couldn't kiss her. The rest of the team watched like last time, but PDA must not be her thing on game day.

"Are you pitching today?"

"I don't know. Probably not." She wouldn't look at me.

"I heard you got a bunch more offers," I said. "But yeah, UCLA must have been pretty impressed with the perfect game." There had to be some combination of words that would unlock this funk. Something to bring back the passion she'd had towards me Friday night. It felt like one of my track dreams where I'm winning a race, but on the home stretch my legs won't move fast enough and I can't get any traction. Instead of winning, everyone else runs by.

"Yeah, I'm not sure what I'm going to do."

"I got my ticket today. I can still get yours if you need."

She finally cracked a smile, but then looked back at the bus. "That's okay. I'll see you at Josh's Friday, okay?"

"All right." We tried to kiss each other's cheeks, but like two drunk Europeans, our timing was off.

"Oops, can we try again?" I said.

She finally looked me in the eyes and smiled. She gave a firm squeeze to both my shoulders. "Mmm-aa," she said, kissing my lips. "You're too good for me." She hopped onto the bus.

I walked to practice staring up at the sky.

24

In second grade our class took a field trip to a fire station. At the end of our visit they asked for one volunteer. Most of us raised our hands, but I was chosen and everyone cheered for me. (It would be a few more years until my intelligence was resented.) Would I get to slide down the pole? Feed the Dalmatian? Maybe fire up the siren one last time? Either way, my career path was chosen.

One of the firemen picked me up. I landed inside two giant boots that pushed against my crotch. A coat that weighed more than me hit my shoulders like a wave. I wobbled as a helmet slammed onto my head. It smelled of smoke and I couldn't see through the mask. Instead, I heard a roar of laughter from my classmates. It was the most uncomfortable outfit I had ever worn. That is, until I put on my tuxedo before prom.

Dad watched me struggle with my cufflinks before finally stepping in. All those extra buttons, the vest, the noose of a tie— why would anyone choose to wear such an outfit?

My biggest mistake was taking such a hot shower on the warmest day of the year so far. My shirt stuck to my back, and beads of sweat raced towards my waist the whole drive to Josh's house. Of course it was over seventy degrees out on the night I had to wear a thick black jacket.

Through the nerves my stomach growled. I turned into Josh's snaking driveway and calculated the nine hours since breakfast.

The house stared at my dad's car as I parked in a driveway that looped in front of a large wooden door. The sun wasn't down yet, but lights from the ground shone up onto the house. I rang the doorbell. A series of chimes erupted from inside.

Josh's mother, Catherine, answered dressed in a black cocktail dress with a glass of white wine glued to her hand. "Don't you look spiffy? Welcome," she said. "The boys are all downstairs, and I don't think any of the ladies have arrived yet." I hesitated, wondering if I needed to remove my shoes, but since they were part of the rental and still immaculate, I left them on.

The house was a cathedral of sorts in the middle. The ceiling must have been three stories high before it sloped down into countless hallways and rooms. Like Andy's house, the thick scent of candles emphasized the cleanliness. I followed Catherine into the kitchen, where the ceiling finally lowered some. Everything was stainless steel. "Beer's in the fridge, hun," Catherine called out. "Help yourself."

"Thanks," I said.

She walked back in. "Oh, and most importantly, those bowls on the counter. Keys go in the left, and take as many as you need from the right."

I dropped Dad's keys into the first bowl. The second bowl had large square wrappers in all the colors of the rainbow. My first guess was candy, so I grabbed a handful and figured it would suffice for my stomach situation, but then I looked closer.

Catherine popped her head back in. The glass of white wine was almost empty. "You boys sure are ambitious," she said.

I shoved the wrappers into my pocket. My face matched the red ones.

A small hallway past the kitchen led to a set of carpeted stairs. It sounded like everyone was yelling.

When I was halfway down the steps, Jefferson spotted me first. "Lender! Catch up!" He wound up to throw a beer at me. I flinched at his bluff, and he laughed. Then his arm was around my shoulder, leading me over to the group. I fit like an incorrect puzzle piece into a half-circle around Bill Harding's recliner.

The basement and its ivory carpet stretched the entire area of the house. I couldn't believe the hundreds of square feet under soft lighting. A cool draft blew from the vent just above me.

"Tribe's down five zip in the second," Bill said with an imported beer in his hand. Compared to our television, he was watching a different game. The monster of a screen showed every wrinkle on the players' faces. The dozen or so speakers made it sound like we were at the ballpark.

"Joshua, your girlfriend is here!" Catherine called down. Our heads turned as the oldest freshman girl of Pond Bridge High strutted down the steps in six pounds of makeup.

Josh picked her up and threw her over his shoulder—I guess as a romantic gesture.

"What the hell's her name again?" Jefferson asked me.

"No idea. They change often."

He leaned in and whispered, "She used to be in our grade, didn't she?"

I nodded and we laughed. Every few minutes another can opened and the conversation got louder. Jefferson put his arm around me again as we reminisced about the basketball seasons from years ago. After touting each other's skills in fifth-grade camp, he slammed the rest of his can. "Hey," he said. "I guess I've kinda been a dick lately."

I nodded yes.

"I just—It's just, I like you better when you don't act like a fucking baby. You know what I mean?" I put my hands in my pockets as he went on. "I mean, seriously, I don't mean to be a dick about it, but, I don't know. You're always so fidgety, and when people are like that, it gets on my nerves for some reason."

167

I absorbed his reasoning and debated whether to forgive him or the alcohol.

"We're cool, right?"

I left my hands in my pockets and nodded.

"The ladies are here!" Catherine hurried down the steps clutching the banister. She stumbled at the bottom before straightening.

"Christ, Cat, don't hurt yourself," Bill said. He splashed beer onto his gray shirt. Dark spots appeared.

Catherine's face gave us the first clue. Her eyebrows shot up at the same time her mouth opened. She lifted the empty glass to her mouth. "First, we have Miss Leah Hayden."

All of us stood there, stupid jealous boys, as the forgotten Hayden sister joined our company in the plush basement. Sometimes silence is the loudest reaction. Her green dress gave her a photoshopped body. Her tan surpassed her freckles, and the little bit of skin showing around her neck teased our eyes.

"G'damn," Josh mumbled. His date elbowed him, but her eyes stayed on Leah too.

I think I heard the television announcer mention a home run, but it could wait.

"And who's this young man coming down next?" Again Catherine sipped from an empty glass.

If she hadn't stunned us into silence, we wouldn't have heard her. "Todd," Leah said.

"Well then, let's welcome the very lucky Todd." Catherine set her glass down and clapped.

The steps alluded to the grown man's weight. A full set of shoulders wore a tuxedo that even Brian would have had trouble filling out. When he got to the bottom of the staircase, the same bald head and blue eyes stared at me first. There was no cropping him out of this situation.

A sour twisting shot through my stomach. Goodbye, hunger; jealousy has no appetite.

Jefferson stepped forward and shook his hand. "Hi, I'm Jeff. Nice to meet you, Todd."

"Thanks, bro." He looked at the can in Jefferson's hand.

"You go to UC?"

"Yep. Finishing up next fall."

"Oh, a fellow Bearcat," Bill said.

"So. High school prom. Cool," Josh said. He usually didn't play sniper with his sarcasm.

Bill handed Todd one of his imported beers and the two began discussing fraternities down in Cincinnati.

"Hun, are you ready?" Catherine looked back up the steps.

"Well wait until I announce you." But Angel was already halfway down the steps.

Despite her promise, my socks were still on my feet.

She wasn't stunning or sexy, but instead gave off a vibe of obligated attendance.

I walked to her, confident that I could coax a smile out, but her expression stayed blank. Her dress was a pale blue, knee-length, see-you-at-church garb. What was wrong with her? Already drunk? Or maybe still hungover? It would take everything I had learned these last few months to turn the night around.

"You look great," I said. I'm not a good actor.

"So do you." She wasn't either.

I leaned in and hugged her. Where was the perfume? "I'll get you a drink," I said. Beer had worked wonders on Jefferson.

"That's okay," she said. A smile forced its way onto her face.

"What's wrong?"

Angel nodded her head towards Leah, but that's all I got.

We stood by each other, her arms folded, while the rest of the dates showed up. Catherine resumed her introductions as the rest of them played along happily.

It wasn't fair. Where was my happy girl?

Once everyone had arrived, Catherine refilled her glass and got the room's attention. "Is everyone ready for corsages and boutonnieres?"

I wasn't. I had heard these words, but never really gotten around to taking care of anything. They don't teach you this stuff in calculus. I could already hear Brian reaming me.

I looked at Angel and apologized with my eyes.

"Don't worry," she said. "I didn't either." We laughed together. My stomach untwisted itself just a bit. A growl reminded me how long it had been since I'd fed it. Maybe if the two of us were the only sober ones, we would have fun that way.

"I like your dress," I said.

"Oh, no. Sorry. My old one didn't fit." She rubbed her hands up and down her sides.

We were ordered upstairs for pictures, so Angel squeezed into her heels.

The deck on the back of the home was another plain of excess. No wonder Josh was always happy. The back yard looked like a forest from a Zelda game. Squirrels played on soft grass below the trees that towered above.

Bill set up a professional-looking camera on a tripod near their grill. Each couple posed in front of the railing for a half-dozen shots. "We'd better hurry while there's still a little light," he said. Other than us, Leah and Todd were the last to be photographed. I watched as she turned next to him and placed her hand on his chest.

I calculated the creepy math of it all. When she'd been in first grade, he was in sixth. While she'd been in seventh grade, he was a senior. I looked at Josh, hoping he'd fire another shot. Instead, he was standing forehead to forehead with his date. Everyone else seemed to be touching.

"Last two," Bill said. "Last but not least."

Angel stood facing the camera. I tried to put my arm around her, but with her heels, she had close to four inches on me. My jacket restrained my arm's range, and I could feel things coming untucked.

"Let me fix you, young man," Catherine said. She straightened my tie and vest, dusted off my jacket, and even used her thumb to spit-wash something off my cheek. "There. Spiffy again."

We posed. Angel and I just put our arms around the other's back. I glanced up to see if she was smiling. No teeth, just a smile.

"I'll bet Mr. and Mrs. Hayden would love a shot of the girls," Catherine said with her hands folded under her chin. Angel rolled her eyes as she joined Leah along the railing again.

Bill was enjoying this. He'd started to say something, but the last few ounces of sobriety censored him.

I looked over at Todd. He was checking his phone, and I wondered if he was as uncomfortable as me. Turns out that he wasn't. While I stood there fidgeting with my thumbs, he walked over between the two girls for a half-dozen shots. "Mom and Dad will want these," he said.

Each of the sisters put an arm around him and turned. I caught Angel looking up into his eyes and for the first time that night, she let out a genuine smile. Her cheek rested against his breast pocket. If she was queen of the world, he was the king.

25

Everyone buzzed about their first limousine ride. Not me. Mine had been the trip to Mom's burial. It had been so spacious and unnecessary for Dad and me. His sisters had taken their own cars. Though not as morbid, it was hard to call this limo ride an improvement. This time it was cramped and a speaker right behind my head deafened me at ninety beats per minute. Angel squeezed my hand once, but let go right away. Every one of her smiles said *I'm sorry, this is the best I could do.*

We were fashionably late to prom, and I was fashionably starving. Inside the Elk Falls Convention Center, more bass boomed off the walls. Lights blinked a spectrum of colors and the scent of dry ice intruded our noses. Balloons in school colors littered a dance floor which was yet to be filled with small-town, teenage rhythm at its worst.

"Looks like we missed dinner," Jefferson said. A busboy cleared the last of the tables nearby.

"Are you kidding? I need to eat," Angel said. At last, some emotion. Forget a corsage, I should have brought her a six-pack of tacos. Her frown remained, and there wasn't anything I could do about it.

"I found you something," Todd said. He held out a basket still wrapped in a white cloth napkin. Angel opened it and let out a squeal when she saw dinner rolls. Somehow Todd had produced a bread basket to feed my date like he was copying that miracle from the New Testament.

The music picked up, and I scanned the long room for Brian. Large huddles started to form, boys to one side and girls to the other. I felt a hard smack on my back. "Your night going as shitty as mine?" Brian said. He looked sweaty.

"How'd it go?" I asked. Maybe I should've warned him.

"She turned it down and said she wanted to take a little break after tonight." The false happiness left his voice hollow.

"You going to be okay?" I looked over at a crowd of girls that included Carissa. Angel joined them, her head above everyone else's like a periscope.

"I guess. She just doesn't know about doing the whole long-distance thing next year. You'll have to discuss the same issue with Angel."

Half-listening, I nodded.

"You've always got your backup," Brian said. He pointed to the far end of the dance floor by the DJ booth. Katy slow-danced with her date. He was a guy Brian and I had nicknamed Wolf a few years ago when he'd started growing facial hair even a year ahead of Brian.

The song ended, and Katy walked towards us. I didn't recognize it at first, but she wore the red dress Angel had tried on for fun. Thankfully, a few safety pins and alterations covered a lot more of her. I figured I'd be polite for the inevitable conversation. Could I tell her she looked nice and keep a straight face? I thought about asking her how she found the dress.

She walked right by us.

"This is weird," I said. "Do I smell or something? Was there a tweet going around saying I had an STD?"

173

"She's just playing hard to get," Brian said. We continued to watch Katy walk up to Leah. They hugged and then Leah introduced Katy to Todd.

"So now they're pals?" I asked.

"They have foods class together first hour. I think they partnered up a couple times."

Katy's body language was only semi-spastic, and her chin was almost in Todd's chest as she spoke to him.

" I guess he now knows about her six nieces and nephews too," I told Brian. Whatever she said, Todd laughed.

Another slow song began and Katy walked back towards her date after giving Todd's arm a firm squeeze. "Save me a dance," she yelled to him.

"We'd better find our ladies," Brian said. He wiped his shiny forehead with a handkerchief, and we walked towards our heartbreakers.

"Ready to dance?" I asked Angel.

"I guess." I followed her over to a spot near Brian and Carissa. She took my hand and held it out at the side. I put my other hand on her hip, and we slowly started turning. I looked around as other couples enjoyed a full embrace. Even Brian and Carissa were a hundred times closer than us.

I felt short. I was meaningless. She looked at everyone but me, and probably made faces to Carissa with each rotation. The song ended and she started to walk away, but I didn't release her hand.

"Did I do something wrong?" I asked. "If this is about the other night, I was just surprised."

She looked me, but just for a moment, and then shook her head. Again I asked what was wrong.

Tears welled up, but they only made her eyes sparkle. I stared into them like they were showing footage of every moment we'd spent together.

"Is it because you're going to school really far away next year? Did I get you in trouble? Is it something with Todd?" I wasn't moving, yet after each guess she felt further away.

She blinked and sent a little river through her makeup on each cheek. She looked just over my shoulder. "I fucked up, Mark," she said, then sniffed. "I ruined everything."

I dropped her hand and watched her walk to the nearest hallway exit. I wanted to tell her it was okay. We weren't official or exclusive yet. Whatever she did, she probably didn't mean it. She had urges, and I just hadn't been ready for her yet. But now I was. I could solve this complex equation.

I could still love her. I would *tell* her I loved her.

The dance music picked up and the huddles formed again back out on the dance floor. Todd masterfully led Leah through spins and dips. She was a yo-yo he could release and return with his giant hands. He had unlocked a smile on her that no one had seen in years. Maybe there was a family curse that said only one sister could be happy at a time. It was Leah's turn.

I needed to tell Brian everything, but he and Carissa were at least talking, so I took a seat on the side of the room and felt sorry for myself. Shortly after, Mr. Mallett approached in the gray suit he normally wore on Tuesdays. He unbuttoned the coat and sat next to me. Was moping illegal too?

He had to yell over the music. "I heard some pretty good stuff about you since the last time we talked," he said.

"From who?"

"A few teachers."

"Well that was my only detention. Ever." Which was worse, sulking alone or chatting with the assistant principal?

"Well, Mr. Pierson didn't exactly leave me a naughty and nice list." Across the room a balloon popped, so he stood up for a moment.

"He would've been able to help. Give him a call next time my reputation's on the line," I said, but Mallett was still investigating from afar.

"I'm sorry, what?"

"Never mind. Good talk."

He nodded and walked away. I sure knew how to scare people out of a conversation. I let the thoughts of Mom numb me like a drug. What did a stupid girl matter compared to what I'd already endured?

It wasn't working, and the disappointment continued.

After four terrible pop songs, the DJ slowed things down again when "Wonderful Tonight" came on. I gazed at my shiny shoes. The spinning lights reflected off of them.

"May I have this dance?" It was Katy, and she said it like someone had instructed her to ask me. I looked around, my insecurities still instinctual, and figured the night couldn't get any worse.

Jefferson saw me, but only gave a half nod. Brian was so focused on pressing his face into Carissa's that he never looked. Never give up, I guess.

I took Katy's hand. She was burning up and her perfume smelled like something an old lady would wear. After two rotations I concluded that Angel wasn't coming back, so on it went. I caught myself looking at everyone but the person with whom I was dancing, just like Angel had done with me.

"You should be proud, Marky," Katy said after the first chorus.

"Thanks," I said with no idea what she meant. It was normal.

"I think I mentioned I have six nieces and nephews," she said with a little emotion creeping into her voice, "but it's too early to tell."

"Huh?"

"But if I had my guess, I'd say it was a boy. He'll be adorable."

With all the algebra, geometry, trigonometry, and calculus I'd done, none of it confused me the way Katy could.

"I think I'm going to go cut in on Leah, and get a dance with her date. He's more my type now anyway." She let go of my hand. "I just can't handle your Samsonite."

"My what?"

"Baggage, Marky. I can't handle it." She took her glasses off and stared at me. "And sorry I used you."

I looked at the floor hoping a trap door might swallow me. Jefferson was no longer oblivious, and I'm pretty sure he mouthed, "That's cold," over his date's shoulder. Josh saw it too and gave me a thumbs up accompanied by a confused look.

I turned to walk back to my seat and was almost there when another hand touched my arm. "That was really nice of you," Leah said. "C'mon."

I went to take her hand, but she put both of hers on my shoulders. Her breath smelled like cinnamon, and I wasn't sure, but I think she was wearing a spray of Ocean Bay. I did my best to control the shaking in my hands as I placed them on the sides of her waist. She felt muscular, but slim compared to Angel. Holding her wasn't so intimidating and overwhelming. My fingers stretched onto the small of her back. She was only a few inches shorter than me, and I looked back and forth from her green eye to her blue eye. She felt perfect in my arms.

"This probably isn't the best place to talk." She looked up. "But you never give me the chance anyway." She said it too fast to sound mean.

I had no response. We both glanced over at Katy, who was hanging off of Todd. His broad smile held a security that no one in their teens can sustain. What did he care if the weirdest girl at our high school liked him?

"Do you know if I did something wrong?" I asked Leah. Her hair was a little messy from her earlier dancing, which somehow made it look better. I tried to push the image of her of walking into that nursery out of my mind.

She laughed a little and shook her head. "Have you not figured it out yet?" She smiled with pain in her eyes. "I thought Katy would've told you sometime this week."

"She said something about having a—" I stopped turning.

Angel wasn't wearing the perfume. Angel was always hungry. Angel called herself hormonal. Angel couldn't fit into her dress anymore. Angel puked in the parking lot. Tonight of all nights, Angel wasn't drinking.

Leah gave me a satisfied nod as her lip curled. Then she walked away. There was something vengeful about the whole exchange.

I looked over at Katy still clinging to Todd. I considered telling her to pass that congratulations on to him.

What do we do now? my heart asked.

26

Someday we would laugh about it maybe. We didn't know then. Having Brian drive me home was not how either of us would have predicted our junior prom to end. His gentleman ways were so engraved that he actually opened the passenger door for me as we got into his grandpa's town car.

"Thanks, darling," I said.

"I'm done with it," he said. "I did everything I could, and if she's not ready to commit, then that's her problem."

I opened my mouth to console him, but he wasn't done. "I'm the only boyfriend she's ever had. Why did she make love to me if she didn't feel the same?" He started the car, but we stayed parked outside the convention center. "I'm going back in." He shut the engine back off.

"No, Brian," I reached over. "Just trust me, that's not the best thing to do right now. I know it sucks, but you're not going to fix it tonight."

"I should at least wait until her dad gets here."

"That's who's picking her up?"

He nodded.

"And you already said your goodbyes?" Knowing what I knew, she was probably going to end up at Josh's.

179

We sat there in silence, though I still heard a faint booming from the music inside. The dome light clicked off after so long, and I thought I heard my friend sobbing. He started the car and turned the stereo up.

"So what happened with Angel?" he asked as we started home.

"Well. She's pregnant," I said.

"You didn't?"

"Course not." I thought back to everything and double-checked that there was no possible way. "It's Todd's," I said. Saying it felt like relief. I hadn't done anything wrong, she had. She'd admitted it. I was a happy victim suddenly. Innocence was my consolation prize. Mom would note that.

"Well that's going to make things interesting," Brian said.

"Yeah, the whole school's going to know soon. Maybe I'll get some sympathy for once." I starting laughing at my misfortune. "And Katy of all people figured it out first."

"How did Katy—Never mind, apparently her sisters get knocked up every nine months."

We passed Josh's house and turned onto Main. I considered telling Brian about Carissa at the party, but the truth wouldn't help anything, so I let him sing along to "Ring of Fire" on the radio.

"So wait," Brian said. "They knew about the pregnancy before tonight, right?"

"I guess. She was absent half the week. I don't know when Katy figured it out, but all the Haydens must know."

"And you said Todd's the father?"

"The water in Cincinnati is fertile. Disgusting, but fertile." It felt so good to make jokes. I earned that right. I was the victim.

"Then why did I see Leah and Todd making out in the hallway earlier?"

It felt like a second blow in the gut. Leah was beautiful and quiet and smart. He couldn't have her too. "What's next? Is this guy gonna steal every other girl in our school? This asshole needs to go back to college."

"Well, he did replace you in Katy's eyes. You owe him that."

Neither of us was ready to go home, but being dateless the rest of the night around our peers wasn't a good plan either. There weren't a lot of options in Pond Bridge.

At Perky's we laughed and joked and whined and bitched for a long time through cups of coffee. The staff dimmed the lights to let us know they were ready to close. Just two losers in tuxedos who'd spent half their prom night at a coffee shop. "What a waste of money," Brian said.

"No kidding. I have to pay my dad back for tickets, Angel's perfume, this tux, and a few other things."

"He let you borrow that much?"

"I'm telling you, anything to do with dating and he's pushing me out the door with his credit card."

"Well let me cover this," Brian said, taking the check.

The caffeine zipped through my veins, and I had never wanted to run so badly. The idea of going from rented shoes that squeezed my feet to my running sneakers thrilled me. I just had to figure out a new route and maybe set a new distance record.

On the drive home, Brian babbled about playing the field and how Carissa would miss him. I absorbed my new role as Mark, the poor victim. He turned down South Street and we were almost to my house when Brian stopped in front of the neighbor's mailbox. "Who's that?" he said.

A small hatchback, I couldn't make out the make or dark color under the streetlight, idled in our driveway. Dad was talking to the driver before he looked up into Brian's headlights. When his attention returned to the driver, I saw his face crumble. The car backed out and drove off the other way.

"Want me to hang around?" Brian asked.

"No, because whatever it is, I didn't do it," I said. I reflected back once again to make sure I hadn't broken any rules. Maybe word got back about the party last week, or even worse, Josh's party tonight. Maybe they'd tried to sneak some drinks into prom and were trying to round up everyone involved.

"You sure?" Brian said.

"Word travels fast in Pond Bridge. He probably thinks I'm going to be a father."

"Well, if the baby comes out with giant ears that don't fit its head, you may have to submit some DNA."

"Very funny." I got out of the car and waved to Brian. Dad stood on the porch with his shoulders slumped. When I joined him he forced an act. "What happened at prom?"

"Who was that? I swear I didn't do anything wrong."

He laughed at me. "Come inside."

The living room smelled different. A cheap candle we kept in the bathroom was down to its final inch on the kitchen counter. The coffee table had a few empty beer bottles on it. It was so late that the baseball game from earlier was being replayed. It was weird to think how the last time the third inning was on I still had hope.

I sat on the arm of the couch while he stood by the kitchen table. He blew at the candle but it only flickered, staying lit.

"Dad, who was that?" My shoes pinched my feet, my tie was a permanent gag, and I had to pee, but none of it was as painful as the look in his eyes.

"That was Carol," Dad said. "We've been out a few times." He sat down in a kitchen chair. Mom's old one.

"Were you going to tell me about her?" My throat swelled.

He shrugged and I was looking at an older version of myself. "No point now."

When I had a therapist shortly after Mom died, she always stayed quiet when she knew I could extend my answer to a tough question. It worked on Dad too.

"She told me I wasn't ready. I thought I was." He stood back up. "I'm not."

I cried. I cried because I felt sorry for him. I cried because I felt guilty that he'd felt guilty enough to hide her. I cried because he was lonely. I cried because I was lonely. He joined me on the couch and handed me a tissue.

"Let's watch the game. I missed it the first time," he said.

So we did. I told him about Angel. And how some guy named Todd had swooped her away from me. And how Brian got dumped. It didn't hurt as bad after so many words. "I guess you have to return that tux tomorrow?" he said. His eyes were starting to shut.

I had kicked my shoes off and loosened the tie a long time ago, but taking everything else off meant it was over and I'd failed. "That soon?" I started to empty my wallet and phone from the pockets. Then I pulled out the four unused condoms.

"Guess it's too late for those," I said, but he was already asleep.

27

Once Dad started snoring loud enough to wake the neighbors, I changed into my running clothes. The air outside was cool, and it felt good at first, but a sweatshirt would've been helpful. I promised myself I'd get the one back from Katy. I settled for a long-sleeve t-shirt and sweatpants and then went outside. Our porch light was still on. The street felt quieter once I shut it off.

I looked up at the half-moon. How much of tonight did Mom witness? Who was she more disappointed in? It was too late to run through the cemetery anyway. I wasn't going to torture myself on Edge Road either. Instead, I just sat there and listened to crickets. A couple of blocks away cars were still driving down Main Street. Probably prom dates that went better than mine.

My body began to play "How long can I just sit here?" I relived every kiss with Angel. I scrolled through her pictures on my phone. I reread all of our texts and emojis. Love was the muddy pair of shoes in which I'd run half a marathon in one night. Could I have done anything differently?

The moon moved through most of the sky, and I totaled the hours since I'd eaten or slept. "Numb," I said out loud. "So this is numb."

A few minutes later headlights appeared at the end of the street. Actually just one headlight. A jolt shot through me, but I stayed on the porch with my feet stuck on the steps. She parked a little farther down under a tree instead of a street light, but didn't get out of the truck. Did she even see me?

I waited. A cloud darkened the moon some more. The silence lasted so long I started to doubt myself. Other trucks could be missing a headlight. Or maybe I imagined it. But then a door slammed shut, and I could hear her walking. Still in the shadows, she paused in the middle of the street. I didn't want to scare her, but then again, she was coming to me.

"Mark?" She said it like she should be the surprised one.

"Hey."

"Can I talk to you for a second?"

What an odd way to ask. She sounded different. An ounce of hope came. Maybe the doctor was wrong. Leah wouldn't kiss Todd if he got her sister pregnant. Maybe we could pick back up where we left off. Was she smiling? The condoms were just inside!

"I'm all ears," I said.

She took a few steps towards me until we could see each other's faces. "What are you doing out here?" She had changed into shorts and her yellow hoodie. She shivered and rubbed her arms.

"Just thinking," I said. Not judging, not insulting, not burning any bridges.

"Sorry I disappeared like that. It wasn't cool of me."

The therapist in me stayed silent again.

"My dress tore, so I was kinda screwed."

Was that it? Her dress tore and she left? I could forgive that. We'd laugh about it with all of our other moments.

"And then Leah wasn't helping much."

"I imagine you two have some things to figure out."

"Not really. I mean, you know how she is. She never really comes out and says anything." She shivered some more.

"Do you want to sit down?" I scooted over, and she joined me on the steps. Her bares knees were higher than mine. "You know

185

what this reminds me of? That time in the cafeteria." We could rewind it all somehow. Memories and words flooded my brain.

"Which one?"

"Right before you kissed me the first time."

Nothing.

She leaned back. "So. . ."

Had Leah actually said Angel was pregnant or was I going on Katy's hearsay? Hope kept creeping in. Maybe Angel had had some anxiety attack. It was her first dance with a date, after all, and her dress had ripped. The pressure of signing a full ride and leading an undefeated softball team had gotten to her, and now she wanted to make it up to me. How clean was my room?

I imagined tomorrow morning. Dad would be reading his Sunday paper and sipping coffee. He'd find an article about Angel's scholarship offer from UCLA and want to tell me about it, but then Angel would walk out of my room instead. We'd have a good laugh and he'd forgive my credit card debt.

"Soooo," she said again. "I'm pregnant."

Fuck you, hope!

"I know," I said. "You couldn't even wear the perfume." I sighed.

"Or drink, or yeah, any of that stuff anymore."

"Why didn't you tell me? I mean, why did we even go tonight?"

She broke eye contact. "I just found out."

"Tonight?" I was too loud.

"No, this week. But I just wanted one more night as a normal girl." I couldn't forgive her even though I felt bad. "You liked me, I think, and no boy has ever asked me to a dance except you. You didn't care that I was taller and fat."

"You're not fat."

"Or care that I'm an Amazon. Or I like to have a good time." She laughed a little. "Most boys get scared away, I guess."

She felt sorry for herself, but that wasn't good enough for me. I knew anything I wanted to say would come out wrong. My mouth didn't care.

"I guess we'll always have to wonder *what if* from now on." She didn't react, so I continued. "I was going to tell you I loved you." Her head dropped onto her folded arms. I had known that would make her cry. It did. We sat there as the sky began to get lighter.

"Why?" she asked.

"You don't know what you did to me, Angel. I thought about you every day from that moment in the cafeteria. I look at those pictures of you on my phone from that day at the mall all the time." Everything spilled. "I hadn't even kissed anyone else and suddenly this beautiful girl is taking her shirt off around me." She needed to hurt as bad as me. "You have to be careful just going around playing with feelings on someone like me who no one pays attention to."

"I wasn't trying to play with your feelings," she said. "When I'm attracted to someone I. . ."

The old married couple who lived down the street drove by. Probably on their way to a sunrise service. "I guess we'll never know," I said.

I figured she had signed up for enough lectures, so I tried to change the subject.

"You hear about Carissa and Brian?"

She nodded. Whatever I said was still sinking in.

"And good luck getting Katy off of Todd."

"He isn't really a concern anymore." She stood and stretched. I looked up to see a sliver of her stomach below the sweatshirt. A second heartbeat had been there all along.

What if?

28

The wind smelled like pig Monday morning. And maybe rain. I'd slept in much later, so instead of jogging north on Main, I ran straight to the cemetery. Even with the clouds, there was more light than I was used to. My shoes made footprints in the damp grass next to her stone. I wouldn't have time to stay long, but I wanted to say something to her. A confession? An apology? Maybe I'd just ask her to look out for me. Would she have warned me about Angel?

I bent down to thumb a cross over her engraved name when I heard a car pulling up. Dad parked behind me and got out. He had his slacks and tie on because he was on his way to work.

We stood there side by side for a minute or two. A few sprinkles touched my cheeks.

"I was coming out here every day," I said. "Until recently."

"Me too." His voice sounded an octave lower.

"I don't know if it makes things easier or harder."

The sprinkles turned into a mist. Dad wiped his cheeks, but left the droplets on his glasses. "I feel like when you see someone every day, nothing changes with them. You can't grow apart." He fought a crack in his voice. "If there's time in between—a few days, a week or two—time grinds your memory down and changes everything you had."

I didn't bother with the moisture on my face. "Do you think she watches us every day?"

He shook his head. I don't know if it was because he didn't know, or his answer was no. It didn't matter. "Every time it rains, I think she's crying," I said. I barely got it out before I was hugging Dad. The raindrops rolled down his waterproof jacket.

Then the rain stopped.

***

I was the first student in Mr. Bates's calculus class. Turns out I was also the last. It was senior skip day. I took my usual seat, third row back, and looked around at all the posters I'd never noticed before. If they created calculus II by next year, this is how it would be for me every day. The bell rang and Mr. Bates entered in stride.

"Alright folks, we'll get started as soon as I take attendance." I admired how he committed to the bit, but I wouldn't smile. He called all two dozen other names out loud and marked everyone absent on his clipboard before finally breaking character.

"Worst weekend of my life and I'm still here," I said. If my peers weren't present to give me sympathy, the duty would fall to my teacher.

"You know, most juniors were skipping today too. Hangovers aren't just for seniors," he said. He was right. Neither Josh nor Brian were planning on showing up. I'd have my pick of seats all day.

For the bulk of the time, Mr. Bates was content to catch up on his grading, while I rested my head on my desk. My next meet was tomorrow, and my sleep schedule was way off because of Saturday night's aftermath. At first I worried that he'd forget to wake me up. What if I didn't wake up until eight hours from now? But fatigue assuaged the fear.

With only a few minutes left I lifted my head and yawned. "Mr. Bates, have you ever finished second in anything really important?"

My teacher paused from his papers and looked at the ceiling. "I did. Junior year. It was the 1600."

"But was it a really big meet?"

"Indiana State Championship."

"That'll work. So afterwards, did you ever think how your life would've been different if that guy who beat you didn't run?"

His forehead wrinkled.

"Like, without him, if he never existed, think how much better that would have been for you."

"If he never existed?"

"Yeah. One arbitrary person ruined it for you."

"This isn't about track, is it?" He sat on a desk in the front row.

"Without this Todd guy, my life would be so much better. I'd have a girlfriend and be happy, but one guy had to ruin it for me. Don't you see the parallel?"

"No."

"If that one runner was never born, you would have won that race. If Todd didn't exist, well. . ."

"Are you going to kill someone?" he asked before laughing.

I stared at him.

"Mark, you know what happened because of that one guy who beat me?"

"He found a miracle cure that ended up saving your life in a happy twist of irony?"

"No. I learned from my loss, trained my ass off even harder, and won state as a senior." He got out of his chair and sat on a desk in the front row. "And whoever got second that day isn't still wishing I didn't exist. They moved past it and tried again."

"Well I don't get a second chance with Angel. Someone named Todd took it from me." His name always earned extra emphasis. "I mean, what, he couldn't stick to girls at his college? He couldn't stick to girls in his hometown? He couldn't even be responsible enough to not get Angel pregnant." At some point I'd gotten out of my seat.

"Everything happens for a reason, Mark."

190

"I've heard that cliché since my mom died. The reason is my life sucks, and anything good in it is taken away from me."

"Well if it makes you feel better, her life is pretty messed up now."

"It's better than being alone. We didn't even make it through prom, and he gets to spend the rest of his life with her so they can live happily ever after."

I was proud of my rant. No one should deny me of my victimhood. I sat back down before Mr. Bates responded.

"Mark." His smirk discounted my emotion. "I know you're hurt, but look at it this way. You lost prom night, but she lost a full ride to UCLA. Her coach told me she had to reject the offer over the weekend."

What that phone call must have sounded like. I tried not to show it, but Bates was right. I wasn't going to tell him. The bell rang, so I got up.

"No one gets love right on their first try," he said as I walked through the door.

I thought about the night Angel and I had a talk about how we both wanted to get out of our boring town. We'd been so sure of our escape. I was going to be so happy wherever we went, just as soon as we got out of Pond Bridge.

I guess if you try to leave too soon, it pulls you back in.

29

The rest of the morning classes were just as lonely. Actually, lonely wasn't the right word. Maybe it was solitude, and maybe I needed to get used to it.

At my empty lunch table, I set my backpack in the chair next to me for company. Only a few dozen other kids were scattered around the cafeteria except for the large table of freshmen in the middle. I took the shell out and sat it next to my tray.

Before I could even unwrap my sandwich, Katy sauntered over and grabbed the chair across from me. She turned it backwards, straddled it and then leaned in. She wore a new pair of glasses, and her hair wasn't as tangled.

"I should tell you that I'm interested in seeing someone else," she said. "It's best you hear it from me."

I opened my mouth to counter her delusion, but before I could she cut me off.

"Plus, I can't keep ruining you for other girls. I'm kidding Marky. I know I never had a chance, but it was fun trying."

She leaned back and almost spoke like a normal person. "It's pretty obvious that since I--well, we started crushing on you, like, all the other girls are copying." If only. "I mean, Marky, you gotta wonder, don't you? Do they really like you, or was it just because we liked you first?" She stretched her hands across the lunch table the same way Angel had the night we ate at the diner. Over me or not, there was still no chance I was touching her paws again. She would have to milk the memory from prom. Instead of taking her hand, I set the shell on her left palm. I looked at it one last time, remembering how it'd meant the world to me when I'd thought it was from Angel. Then I silently cursed it for tricking me into spending all that money on perfume.

"You should have this back," I said. "It was a nice gesture and all, but it looks—"

"You realize that isn't mine," she said, pulling her hands back. The shell sat between us, its mystique robbed by circumstance.

"You didn't put this in my locker a few weeks ago?"

"No," she said. "Look, for someone who thinks he's so smart, you sure don't know a thing about—"

"Did you buy me a hot chocolate once at a track meet?"

"Marky. Baby. You're making this hard, but you've got to let it go." She sighed. "Or maybe we can still make this work, if my other men aren't receptive to my love. I'd hate to fight with Leah over another man, but it seems that's where it's headed."

I looked back at the shell. Was it smiling at me? "Hold on," I said. "I just need to know if that was you who bought me a hot chocolate at that one track meet. Remember? You gave it to Josh's dad to give to me after my race?"

"Look, I didn't even know Josh *had* a dad."

Confused, I picked the shell back up. Katy continued to babble about how I needed to make up my mind and either commit to her or not, but her voice disappeared like a frequency that no longer came in.

Sometimes during a really hard calculus test, I'll only have one problem that I'm stuck on. Everything else on the paper comes so easily, but there's always that one problem where I overlook a minor detail, or assume my methods were correct earlier in the equation. I erase everything I thought I knew, adjust the angle of the paper, and then try again. After that, it usually clicks.

193

I pressed the same mental reset button right then. Did she say she was fighting with Leah for me?

I left my backpack and my tray on the table. Katy was still talking, I think. Carrying the shell in my hand, I walked right past Mr. Mallet. He turned to say something, but let me go unencumbered.

I quickened my pace and then froze as I got to the door of the ambassador's office. Instead of knocking, I opened it slowly and peeked in. I heard Leah typing before I saw her. Even after I entered, she didn't look up. It was like she had blinders on.

"Sorry I was too stupid to figure it out." The keyboard stopped clicking, but she still didn't turn around. The styling and curls from Saturday had been straightened out of hair. It fell all the way down her back.

"And the hot chocolate too. That was, um, really nice of you." I wasn't prepared.

"You're welcome," she said. If she hadn't stopped typing, I may not have even heard her. I tried to think of something to say that was better than sorry. Something that would make her forget I ever had anything to do with her sister.

"Why her instead of me?" she asked.

I wanted to tell her she was prettier than Angel. That we were much more alike. We would be perfect together.

I wanted to tell her how Angel had done all the work. Angel initiated everything. She made it *évident*.

"I just—" I went to my memory bank. "Remember that time when we were kids and Brian told everyone we were a couple and they all teased me? Well I remember how upset you were, too."

"Brian didn't start that rumor," she said finally, facing me from her chair. She had on gym shorts and a t-shirt during a school day for the first time ever. A quick smile flashed on her face, like when a boxer takes a solid jab. "I was crying because of how upset you were. *I* started it."

"I didn't—"

"When someone likes you, they don't make it obvious when they should, I guess."

It wasn't the advice she had given me weeks ago; it was a message.

"Well here I am. Making it obvious to you," I said. Brian would be so proud. "I know it's a little soon, but—"

"You're not ready, Mark. You still care what people think too much. I watched you throw out the cookies Katy and I made. You dumped the hot chocolate. Did you give her credit for my note too?"

It had said Mark, not Marky.

"You don't feel that way about me, Mark. If you had, you would've felt it sooner."

"Give me a chance," I said. "I've learned a lot these past few months."

"From my sister? You think I can just forget that? I'm sorry, but I've found someone who's ready." She straightened a few papers on her desk for no reason.

"Well it can't be Todd." She was too smart to share a man with her sister.

She nodded that it was.

"You can't date him. I mean he's going to be a— I mean, Angel. . ." Why did I have to spell this out?

"It's not Todd's baby," Leah said.

Did she think it was mine? What had Angel told her? This rumor was going to be my next round of humiliation if it wasn't cleared up.

"Then who the hell's baby is it?"

Leah took a deep breath and looked at the door. Her silence made me realize how loud I had been. She shook her head like she didn't want to say anything, and then inhaled again. Finally, she released the information that truly showed me I knew nothing. Nothing about anyone close to me. Nothing about emotions or love. A 4.0 was meaningless.

I was still a dumb, dumb little boy.

She stood up, moving towards the door. "Why do you think Mr. Pierson lost his job?"

She walked out as I sat frozen in the office.

THANK YOU

Thank you so much for reading my book. It means the world to me that you spent hours of your life to support my passion in writing. I continue my career as an author because of interest from readers like you. Please feel free to leave a review and reach out to me at RobDurhamComedy.com.

Made in the USA
Columbia, SC
25 April 2018